In and Out of Wonderland Through The Rabbit's Hole
(A Working Title)

By Donnie Rust

The Lost Executive Ltd.

www.thelostexecutive.com

Copyright D.A.A Campbell 2019 ©

Cover images: Canva.

All rights reserved. Except as permitted by author no part of this publication may be reproduced, distributed or transmitted in any form or by any means, or stored in a database of retrieval system without prior written permission of the publisher.

The Lost Executive.com

www.thelostexecutive.com

KDP ISBN: 9781688385276

" With heaps and piles and large mountain ranges of gratitude and thanks to Alexandra Brown. You're epic."

-Donnie Rust

"Once again, I would like to state for the record, everything written here is still, absolutely true."

-Donnie Rust

1.

It was Tuesday and I was fighting a monster.
You'd recognize the sort: tall and lumbering, a patchwork of body parts brought to life through the power of lightning, clever surgery and a stolen reanimation elixir.
It swatted its mad-cap-scientist's head out of the window into the street, picked me up bodily and threw me across the laboratory into a cabinet of beakers, bottles and jars.

Bolts of lightning scoured the sky, immediately followed by the tremendous rolling of thunder as the biggest storm Purgatory had ever seen squatted directly over our heads and prepared to relax its bowels.
I crawled to a nearby refrigerator and crouched behind it. With a breath, I tried to pry a slither of glass that had pierced my abdomen and was busy tickling my liver. My phone rang in my pocket and I pushed the answer button on my handsfree at my ear with a knuckle.

"Hello." I grimaced, as my bloodied fingertips kept slipping off the edge of the glass sticking out of me.

"It's me," my personal assistant said, uninterestedly, "Are you finished yet?"
I looked at the table in the middle of the room which had four very large leather straps dangling from one side where they had been ripped off. Mismatched footprints through the blood around the mad-scientist's headless body, led into the very dark shadows.

"Not yet."

"Hurry up, would you?" Danielle asked, "I want to go home and you said you'd have this wrapped up fast."

"There have been some developments." I hissed through clenched teeth as I managed to dig into the wound and get a fingernail around a jagged front edge of the glass. I sighed with relief when it was out of me and said, "You know Crazy Kevin?"

"Yes." She said, even more uninterested.

"He stole the elixir from Nicholas Flamel and used it in his experiment."

"Case closed then; Mr. Flamel will be delighted. Can you come back to the office now?"

"No. I need you to do some research for me. You know the case that Box asked us to investigate, the one regarding those grave diggings and those missing persons?"

"Yes." She said, sounding more interested now that I'd mentioned Inspector David Box.
I opened the refrigerator and peeked inside, "Yeah, that was all Kevin. He's been stealing body parts for a while now."

"And the missing persons?"

I closed the refrigerator in disgust, "They're not missing anymore but some of their parts are more alive than others."

"You said that Kevin used it on one of his experiments? Which one?"

Crazy Kevin had been an active amateur scientist for some time and had built up quite a reputation for being determined. Even before he became a permanent resident in Purgatory, he had launched himself at the field of science with the idea that enough enthusiasm would produce results. In that respect he wasn't wrong.

"Kevin finally succeeded in making a monster."

"I don't believe it," she said.

"Judging by how he reacted, neither did he," I pointed out, "I don't think he knew what he was stealing when he broke into The Alchemist's laboratory."

One of the glass vials from the cabinet had rolled across the tiled floor to where I crouched. I picked it up and read the label. "Looks like body parts weren't the only thing he was collecting. I'm holding a potion from that other case, regarding the Ladies of Thatch."

"The witches?"

"Yes. This one apparently can help retain a tan for six months. Boring."

"Don't go mucking about with any evidence," Danielle said.

"Of course not," I said in reply, while pocketing the beaker and crawling over to the felled cabinet to see what else was there.

The monster screamed, right behind me. It was a horrid sound, pained and shrill. I spun around in shock to face it as it ran towards me on three of its limbs, trailing sparking power cables and wet tubing.
Lightning flashed outside, painting the laboratory and all its horror in bleached white light and the rage and anguish within the monster's eyes shone out of its sockets. I dropped to the side and stuck my foot out at the last instant to catch the creature's ankle and trip it up. It had not had much balance anyway and collided, like an avalanche of meat, into yet another shelf of breakable items.

Kevin, while not possessing a shred of credible scientific intelligence, had certainly made up for it in commitment to the role. His laboratory was a rat's maze of shelves bedecked with vials and long coiling loops of tubing that connected hundreds of bubbling beakers full of colourful chemicals and sparking tesla coils. Above us a lightning conductor rod of iron and copper wire buzzed disconcertingly while thick cables snaked across the floor bundled together with shoelaces.

"Three cases in one evening, I'll admit that's good going." Danielle said in my ear.
The monster thrashed and howled with inconsolable rage as it struggled to get to its feet and started throwing beakers of acid at me.

"Are you doing filing?" I asked indignantly.

"I'm being productive," she said, coldly, "I know you won't do any of your paperwork. Why are you so out of breath?"

"I'm currently fighting the monster that Crazy Kevin created. Did I not mention that?"

"No. You neglected to mention that. Damnit, fine, what do you need?"

"Well," I said, getting up and peeking again, "I am having a bit of a – shit."

The monster was gone. Cables overhead spasmed and offloaded a shower of sparks onto the destroyed shelves. On the ground bloody cables snaked and coiled malevolently as they sought for their monster.

Also, Kevin's body was missing. There was now just a large puddle of blood with no body lying in it and more mismatched footprints crossing over the previous trail.

"Terrific," I muttered, "Danielle, how do I kill the monster?"

"Bear with," she said, her voice echoing as she put me on loud speaker, "I'm just searching now."

"Take your time."

"I'm trying to find out - be patient!"

The darkness around me was so thick it could have been scooped up in a jug. In it, chains hung from the ceiling and rattled ominously, water dripped, things sparked giving brief, intermittent splashes of light that were soon snuffed out. But inside it there was the sound of labored breathing; wet, angry and hateful.

"Danielle..." I urged.

"Okay, okay, the elixir of Nicholas Flamel can grant life, in large enough amounts even grant immortality. How much was the monster given?"

Somewhere in the darkness I heard a wet crunching sound that made me think of a burrito with chicken bones being crushed in a mulcher: the unique sound created by a combination of wet flesh being perforated and bones being split.

"All of it," I said, "I imagine all of it."

"Ah." she said, "Hold on."

An ear-shredding screech from my left flank made me jump and the monster bounded from the darkness with the stringy remains of Kevin hanging from its broken and mismatched teeth. Blood spilled from the gaps in its cheeks where the flesh had sealed over. In all this mess, its combination of bloodshot and egg yolk yellow eyes was wild with destructive anger.

I screamed in surprise, took a second to select one of the glass vials and threw it at the monster's gap-filled maw.

The vial shattered against its rotten rear molars and spewed the potion down its throat. The effect was immediate.

"Punch yourself in the face!" I commanded.

Without hesitation the monster balled up both its fists, one of them twice the size of the other and started punching itself in the chin and face.

"Don't worry Danielle," I said smugly, "I've sorted the situati- oh shiiiit!"

As the vial had contained a potion that instantly made the drinker a slave to commandments, the monster was doing a very thorough job of punching itself in the face. But with its limbs being different lengths it had managed to capture me in one of its arms en route to punching itself, hence I was caught between its face and its fist.

I panicked, selected another vial without looking first and shoved it into the thing's mouth.

Instantly, as if unfolding out of itself, it turned into an octopus and *really* started punching itself in the face.

"Are you still alive?"

"Yes," I told her, "But so is the monster. I don't think I can kill it."

"Why not?" she asked, "The contract says either find the elixir or destroy it. Nicholas can make more but he doesn't want it falling into the wrong hands. Can I hear drumming?"

"Yes, you can. But listen I have an idea about how to get around this."

"We have spoken about this; you need to stop having ideas."

"Why?"

Just then the potions ran out and their effect reversed as fast as it had occurred, and I cleared six feet in a single surprised step.

It glared at me, its black and blue eyebrows dancing at the current of thought, its blackened lips worked, its blue steaked tongue snaking out and getting in the way of its teeth before it managed to shape a word, "*Why?*"

"Oh my God," I gasped, "You can talk?"

"*Why?*" it said again, its face twisting and contorting into a corpse smile of delight, it took a breath and said, "*Why? Whywhywhywhywhy!*"

"Oh my God. You can intonate too?" I corrected.

It sprang to its feet, spread its hands and started dancing around merrily, flinging its limbs willy-nilly and spinning with delight, dancing like a princess on a podium. Flinging bits of itself here and there with joyous abandonment all while shouting at the top of its mismatched lungs:

"Whywhywhywhywhywhywhywhywhy!"

2.

Nicholas was not happy.

"You have not fulfilled your contract so why should I pay you?" he demanded angrily, slapping his knee and dislodging a small cloud of sulphur from his trouser leg.

Sitting behind my desk I didn't answer immediately as I was preoccupied with making mental notes of all the places he had been in my office. The man had a tendency to leave trails of dried chemicals wherever he went.

"Your elixir has given life and consciousness to someone," I explained delicately, "You have to appreciate that while I was happy to destroy an experiment, I cannot euthanize an intelligent creature."

From the basement we could hear the loud and very merry chanting of, "Whywhywhywhywhywhywhy.... Why!"

Nicholas cocked a dusty eyebrow and folded his arms.

"I'm not a murderer."

"No, murderers don't get paid. You are an assassin," he pointed out.

"I never graduated." I said, "Look, the way I see it the first half of the contract has still been met. You have your elixir downstairs. You can get samples when you need them."

"I don't need samples," Nicholas tutted haughtily, "This is not the 17th century anymore my dear boy - I have revolutionized the alchemy industry and made hundreds of Philosopher Stones. I do not need anything as trifle as *samples."*

Danielle entered then with coffee on a tray. Nicholas beamed a great big smile at her. His teeth were the cleanest thing about him, like a streak of porcelain white in a plate of curry powder. Danielle returned the gesture as she headed out. After a pause Nicholas sighed.

"I miss that," he said.

"Miss what?" I asked conversationally, taking a sip of my coffee.

"Immortality comes at a price," he said in a snotty tone, "You must be willing to make sacrifices. By the time I had invented the Philosopher Stone and made the Elixir of Life, I was already an old man - and certain... preoccupations had gone unexplored. They were beyond me."

The spray of coffee from my mouth didn't reach him but it covered a good portion of the desk.

"But you look so young under... well, all that science stuff...?"

"Appearance is not everything. Certain things are not a prerequisite of life," he said, "I was made young again but there were certain mechanics that had been so forgotten by that time that they remained forgotten."

I cleared my throat.

"But you still... want to?"

"Of course, man!" he snapped, standing up and waving an arm in exasperation, "Of course! What man wouldn't? Especially in this day and age when the women are so available. When I was a lad you had to woo a woman, speak to her father, negotiate terms and propose marriage before you had the chance to see what shade the carpet was compared to the drapes and even then, you could have been surprised but stuck with it. It was so much work and that's why I never got around to doing much about it. I was a scientist. I thought I was content with my mission in life. But now that I have achieved it, I realize there are many things I have missed."

Nicholas sat down and raised a cloud of dust, in which he looked thoroughly depressed.

"You know," I said, reaching over and passing him his coffee, "When I fought the creature last night, I couldn't help but notice that Kevin had been specific on what he was trying to create."

He cocked an impatient eyebrow, "Oh?"

"I had the opportunity to see it and it seemed that while Kevin may have been a total klutz, he had been fairly fastidious when it came to the biology and anatomy of his creation. He had been stealing corpses for months and I think he was wanting to be as generous as he was able to. That monster downstairs is very gifted."

"So, what?" Nicholas said with a shrug, "I've lived in Purgatory for centuries, I have seen many unique and bizarre monsters."

"Yes..." I said, leaning on the corner of the desk, "But he had been made of dead flesh and the parts were... how can I put this delicately... very much alive. Dead flesh, brought back to life, Nicholas. And when I say life, I mean they were very much alive."

His eyes took on a gleam, "You mean?"

I nodded solemnly.

"That monster had a …?"

"He had more than he needed," I said, "It was positively lance-like."

"Is that so?"

"Well, what can I say?" I said, walking over and closing the door to the office. I cast Danielle a quick glance and once shut I waited for Nicholas to turn around in his chair and look at me before I continued.

"Nicholas, imagine it… that creature down there could be the answer to a lot of problems, not only yours but for millions of people. You've turned lead to gold, turned age to youth, why not give people something else to look forward too. After all, what is youth if not the quest for a deep connection?"

He rubbed at his chin, flaking off some of the white powder there, "How… impressive… was it?"

I gave him a modest smile and walked around the side of my desk, I leant on it with both hands and looked him in the eyes, "I would owe a lot to the man who got me that hard."

Outside the office Danielle choked.

"I should rephrase that," I said hurriedly, not wanting to lose the moment.

"No, no," Nicholas said, "I *like* it. This is spectacular! A new opportunity and I owe it to you. Please, forgive my rudeness earlier, I did not see the possibilities. Here."

He took out from his robes a dusty leather purse and dropped it on the desk. Golden coins spilled out.

"When can I take the monster?" he asked.

In one fluid movement I swept the bag of coins into the middle drawer of my desk and raised a finger, "I did not spare that monster's life just to hand it over to another scientist. Your research will be conducted fairly and unequivocally painlessly and Why will be paid for his time. Do we have an accord?"

"Of course," Nicholas said, "I'm sure we can come to some sort of agreement on this matter. Will you be handling the contract?"

"No," I said, "Madam Thankeron will be doing that."

Even through the layers of powders on his face I saw the flesh pale significantly at the mention of that name. His bottom lip trembled as he sought to say something as his mind panicked and deleted any and all schemes and underhanded plans that had been processing. He swallowed hard against a dry throat and croaked, "Very good."

"Please see Danielle before you go and she will give you a receipt," I said, "And we will be in touch to discuss your visits with our mutual friend."

Nodding like a dashboard toy Nicholas Flamel left my office. It took hours before the smell of him left the building though.

Madam Thankeron agreed to meet me that afternoon at the Thankeron Estate which still represents one of the most densely-folded areas of Purgatory. A beautiful modern house made of counter-leveraged concrete slabs and glass walls surrounded by a tall wall that has no end and an equally unending garden that encircles the property and is home to the kind of creatures that need to be kept between trees and behind high walls.

As I approached her front door, I saw beneath the perpetual twilight that hovers above the estate that the gardens were filled with frolicking nymphs dancing around a satyr that was tied to a pyre. Each of the nymphs held in their left hand a long ribbon that they were gleefully winding around the otherwise, tightening the gagged goat man to the wooden post. In their right hands each held a torch that was aflame. Meanwhile, another pair of nymphs were merrily blowing into reed flutes and creating an eerie music. It did not look like a game that all the participants would find fun.

I reached the steps to the front doors when they opened up silently on oiled hinges and an exceptionally tall and scarecrow thin gentleman in a black suit stood before me. Above the collar and thin black tie and below the tall top hat was a face as featureless and as pale as a marble slab save for the pinched smiling mouth and those long, disturbingly straight teeth.

"Detective," the creature said with a small bow.

"Are you the same Slender Man butler that I impaled to that door with an iklwa?" I asked as I neared.

"Yes sir," the Slender Man said charmingly.

"No hard feelings then," I said mounting the steps and shoving passed, "The boss in?"

"Madam Thankeron is in the library waiting for you sir," the butler said, "I shall walk you up."

The interior of the Thankeron Estate had been completely renovated following the last time I visited. The room to room aquarium had been replaced by an endless and very complicated water feature. As the butler walked me through the corridors and passed the many rooms, I followed the working of the water features as the liquid travelled through hundreds of different moving parts. It poured into number of jars, overflowed, touched on leveraged-seesaw bamboo holders that, when filled, deposited the water into more jars. Set up like an endlessly active clockwork that was mesmerizing and quite calming. Steampunk machinery was quite trendy in the city at the moment, I had no idea that Madam Thankeron was such a follower of fashion.

The butler brought me to a large sliding door which he pulled open revealing a chamber larger than the house that held it. A central space surrounded by six floors of shelves stacked to the limit with book spines. At the far end in front of a blazing hearth with a fire in it, sat Madam Thankeron in a high-backed burgundy Chesterfield.

"The former ambassador is here to see you Ma'am," the butler announced.

"Thank you," she said, "Please come in,"
I stepped in and heard either the door or the butler hiss as it slid closed behind me. I took a moment and turned around in a full circle looking at the size of the place, "I've never seen so many books in one room," I said.

"You should have a look at the Book Worm's cavern," she said, closing the book she was reading with a snap.

Lilith Thankeron is not a very tall woman, but she looks it. Long dark hair pulled back from her highly-refined face, a figure-hugging dress of flowing grey silk seductively floated over her distracting curves. As I approached, I noticed that the tattoos that covered her whole body from toe to hairline in red lines and twirls had changed shape. What had been flowing curves had become rigid and square giving her a look as if someone had drawn a highly vexing maze upon her body.

"I see the décor isn't the only thing that has changed," I commented.

"This and that is due to that little favour you did for me," she said, "The water must flow through more jars now, I mechanized it and the tattoos followed suit."

"I can't pretend to understand it all," I said honestly, still approaching across the library floor to reach her.

When I was within reach, she took my hands and smiled up at me, "I always forget how tall you are."

"I always imagine you being taller," I said, with a grin, "How are you Lilith?"

"Endlessly occupied," she said with a shrug, "I was delighted when you said you wanted to meet."

"I hope it hasn't caused trouble?"

"On the contrary, I knew I could rely on you being late which gave me the chance to catch up on some of my reading. Your call seemed urgent?"

She guided me to a smaller single leather seat next to her towering Chesterfield and I sat myself down. I was not surprised to find a decanter of fresh water at hand with two glasses. I took it and poured two drinks, handing one to her. She accepted it with a worried smile, "This must be serious if you're following protocol."

"I have a favour to ask of you," I said.

"Oh, how delightful. Please, go on," she said, sipping her water. I tried some of mine and found it intensely invigorating. Purity of a different level to something poured out of a tap.

I told her about Kevin's monster as well as what the alchemist's elixir had done to it and ended the tale with admitting that to placate Nicholas Flamel, I had totally implicated her in the management of Kevin's monster. Her response was as expected.

"You're such a dick,"

I put the glass down on the table, and looked into the fire, "Lilith, I couldn't kill this creature. It is intelligent but it falls outside the realm of the Embassy who would usually deal with it and the arrangement I have made with Flamel means that this poor creation is safe only as long as you are there to maintain the contract."

"You could have done me the courtesy of asking me first," she said.

"I know that, but you may have said no," I explained, "I had a life to protect and are you not the Mother of Monsters?"

She gave me a sour look, "I cannot wait until you live long enough for people to start making myths and legends up about you."

"I doubt I'll live that long," I said.

She looked at some of my scars that were not covered by my suit. Namely, the round, slightly star-shaped lump of flesh in the middle of my forehead, "It was a generous token that the Devil helped seal the back of your skull, wasn't it?"

Unconsciously, I ran my hand over the back of my head, as if checking my hair cut, "Okay you have a point," I admitted, "But please let's not change the subject. I need this – creature - to be protected."

"And how do you foresee me being able to do that?"

"Let it stay here," I said, "It will be safe and it will be able to learn about this world where it has a better chance of being accepted. Also, Flamel will be less likely to try anything untoward if he knows that the monster is your ward."

"You know I am aware you made that deal so that you could still be paid?" she said.

"I know," I admitted, "I'm not proud of it, but nevertheless I have expenses. Will you help or will you doom Kevin's monster to wander the world, alone, fearful and dangerous?"

"Don't be dramatic, off course I'll help," she muttered, "However."

She fixed me with her steely eyed gaze that could have bleached my shadow to the wall, "In return I need something from you."

I stood immediately and walked away. I returned a moment later with a tumbler filled with straw brown coloured liquid in my hand, "I thought I needed something a bit stronger for this part."

She stared with consternation at the drink and leaned an elbow on the arm of her chair to look behind me.

"You were saying?" I prompted, sitting down and making myself comfortable, "You have my full attention."

"Yes. I should really apologise; I was actually about to contact you myself when you reached out to me. You see, I have dropped you in it as well. Do you know Alice?"

I swigged the drink back in one neck-breaking jerk and threw the tumbler into the fire where it shattered in the flames.

"I see you do." She observed, "Very good. I've never been a fan of making introductions. She needs some help in a little expedition and I told her that I knew the perfect person to help."

I gave Lilith as long and as hard a gaze as I could, "Expedition? Where?"

Madam Thankeron gave me a pearly white smile and for a moment her tattoos blazed as if picking up the firelight, "To Wonderland."

3.

"Why? Why!" the creature was happily trying out every variant of the word, *"Whywhywhywhywhywhywhywhy whyyyyyyyyy.... Why!"*

Why sat on an upturned steel bucket in the middle of the basement, singing merrily to himself while swaying from side to side. It was a scene made all the creepier by how inhuman this creature of human parts looked. It bore to point the fact that Kevin, deep down, had never expected his experiment to actually work. The misshapen mishmash of body parts from as many as nine formerly deceased people had created something far more unsettling than the sum of the parts. And now that I had time to properly look at him, I was truly taken aback by what I saw.

His right arm was highly muscular, bulging out at the shoulder with deeply-striated deltoids, these were woven into a collection of muscular slabs and knots that made up the biceps and triceps. This led into a forearm shaped like a horse's thigh and ended with the gnarled, callused paw of a lumberjack.

In comparison, his left arm was dainty and almost feminine in appearance, ending politely in a much smaller, unlined hand. This was the main reason why, when Why ran, he did so on three limbs while this arm stuck out to the side.

One of his legs was black and the other white, both possessing their own unique musculatures. The black leg was clearly that of an athlete and the other that of a couch potato. Great big, ugly stitches flew across the torso like railway tracks outlining the great patches of flesh that did not match.

Of the many questions Why would be asking, why he had five nipples was no doubt going to crop up. It was his face that gave me the most pause. Every part was a different tone, a different shade and even the skull looked like it had been stapled together without much design. It was beyond me how, clearly having some skill as a grave robber, Kevin had completely failed to find at least one skull that was intact.

Why was truly nightmarish, and calmly sitting in my basement singing to the light bulb that burnt above him.

"You unintended monster," I whispered, "I don't envy you one bit."

At the top of the stairs the door opened, and Danielle called down, "Madam Thankeron has arrived."

"Thanks for letting me know," I called back up, "You can send her down."

A woman appeared in the basement doorway. Tall with a threadbare baseball cap and earthy brown overalls, she started walking down the stairs and I asked, "And you are?"

"Sarcasm is the lowest form of wit." She muttered.

"Just by level then Madam Thankeron," I said with a smirk as she reached the bottom.

"Yes, you are positively a bottom feed- oh my goodness."

Her surprise only lasted a second, but within that moment the monster had stopped singing and both of its horrible bloodshot eyes glared openly at this newcomer. One first, the other took a second to navigate its way around its socket.

"*Why?*" he growled, spit flying out between the gravestone teeth.

"Maybe you should leave." I said, stepping forward but she put a hand to my chest to stop me. Without taking her eyes from Why she took the cap off and the monster's entire demeanour changed as if mesmerized by the thick cascade of her hair tumbling over her shoulders.

"Maybe you should introduce us?" she suggested.

"Why, this is Madam Thankeron."

The monster sucked in his blackened lips and looked from me to her several times. His dainty left hand pointed a manicured finger at her while his right hand anxiously crushed the rim of the bucket like cardboard, "*Why?*"

I nodded and said, "Yes, she's a friend. She is going to keep you safe."

"*Why?*"

I took Madam Thankeron's wrist and walked her forward to the monster who eyed her suspiciously. As we neared him in the cramped basement, he noticed her hair again and became transfixed as if it were the most beautiful thing he had ever seen. He adjusted the way he sat on the bucket.

"Oh my!" she gasped, putting a shocked hand to her mouth. She looked away and for the first time in all the years I had known her, she blushed, "He is gifted, isn't he?"

"That part clearly likes you," I said.
She blushed??

"Why, you see?" I said with a smile, "You can trust Madam Thankeron right?"

"I don't think he's interested in trusting me," Madam Thankeron pointed out, a tiny grin pinching her cheeks.

"Yeah, I do think you should maybe leave," I suggested, "I'll go upstairs and get a bucket of ice water or something and we can try this again in half an hour or so."

"Pish posh! Don't be ridiculous," she muttered with a flutter of her hand, "I know how to handle monsters. I think that you should leave instead."

"No, no, no, that's a terrible idea, Lilith," I said, "This isn't one of your ..."

"One of my what?" she asked, turning to face me, "One of my tame little monsters or one of my cute little fuzzies-wuzzies? I've been dealing with beasts and brutes since before your ancestors thought about wiping their arses with anything other than their hands, so don't question me again, Nooseman. Either get out or stay and watch. But if you do stay, keep out of my way."

Half an hour later Madam Thankeron walked out of the basement with Why walking obediently at her heels.

"Please remind your employer that he must now uphold his side of the deal." she said to Danielle. The pair walked out of the office and down the stairs and out the front door. Why even opened the back door to the limousine himself and climbed in as obediently as a child. Then, just like that, they left.

Danielle found me at the bottom of the stairs, hugging myself and staring at the opposite wall.

"Dare I ask what it is that she did down there?" Danielle asked, handing me an unusually hot cup of coffee.

"I don't... ever... want to speak of it." I said slowly. Taking the coffee in hand and bringing it to my lips, weakly, I asked, "Any phone calls?"

"Actually yes," she said, producing her iPad from thin air, "A woman named Alice called. She said that she's ready to meet you at the corner of Opie Street and London Street."

I swallowed all the coffee and stared at the ceiling.

"Shouldn't you wait just a little bit longer before going out?" she asked.

"Thank you for the concern," I said, "But I won't lie I'm finding it super creepy."

"It's mostly lip service," she said with a nonchalant shrug, "And I'm gunning for a raise."

I was still staring at the ceiling.

"I don't know much about this Alice," she admitted, sitting down at her desk and scrolling through her iPad with an index finger, "I know she's a bounty hunter, has a bit of a reputation for being unorthodox and ruthless. Is it true what it says she did to the Coolbaugh boys?"

"Yup," I said hauntingly, still staring at the ceiling, "With their own clubs too."

She shivered, "That's horrible."

"Some would say that they deserved it," I said, "Like their thirteen victims."

"If she is so capable, why on Earth does she need your help?"

"I know Wonderland better than she does," I said.

Danielle's eyebrows went up, "You know Wonderland better than Alice?"

I took in a deep breath and slapped my chin to get myself in the right frame of mind. Looking in the office's full-length mirror I straightened up my tie and explained, "Well, I went there after she did and I know all the... other places."

"You've been to Wonderland?"

"Yes indeed."

"What's it like?" she asked.

"It's different to what you would expect. I didn't go to the same places that Alice went to you see. I went to the other places."

"And those are?"

"The places that a pre-adolescent girl would be unlikely to visit," I said, "That's why Madam Thankeron suggested me. That, and I think she has a cruel sense of humour."

"Go on, why does this one hate you then?"

I told her and her face became visibly wooden, before she said, "You're such a dick."

4.

Like a film of black vacuumed plastic, all of Purgatory clings to the corners, gaps and alleyways of Norwich. In this old city, at the intersection of Opie Street with London Street is the entrance to Wonderland. You really have to know where to look for it or fall into it blind drunk. That works too.

It was night and the shops were closed and shuttered. The streets bathed in the lonely amber light of empty cities and as I walked to the entrance, I could hear the distant bells that sometimes tolled around the city at odd times. I turned the corner and spotted the entrance and gulped. I had, since leaving that place, not once thought about returning. Like the doorway to an ex's house, you may have to pass it every day but if you don't look at it, it doesn't necessarily exist.

Standing at the entrance were two figures. One of them a huge, hulking mass that towered over the other while still somehow seeming smaller. This other was Alice.

She turned to look at me as I approached. Raven hair framed a pale face dominated by searing green eyes. The combination of ripped black jeans, buckled boots and a black vest top could have made her look demonic if not for the blood red hooded cape that draped across her shoulders and matched the shade of her lips. Few people were aware that the inspiration behind Lewis Carrol's novel and the European fairy-tale of Little Red Riding Hood was based on the same long-lived bounty hunter. Beside her stood a gigantic wolf the height of a grizzly bear who, upon seeing me, snarled with rage and charged at me. There was a snap of a chain and spittle flew from those massive gleaming teeth as his attack was brought to a yanking halt.

"Kaben, heel." Alice commanded.

Growling threateningly, Kaven stood to his full height, steam puffing out from the sides of his massive jaws, yellow eyes blazing against the night sky. After a moment he walked away and went to sit next to Alice.

"I won't lie, I am impressed, Nooseman," Alice remarked, "Most people would not have stood their ground the way you just did."

I smirked, "It was nothing."

She turned back to the door and I put my hands on my knees.

"Kaben is usually much calmer," she said, "I'm glad I caught him in time, I'd hate if the two of you started on the wrong footing,"

"What about our footing?" I enquired, joining them so that Alice was between us. Kaben glowered at me vehemently.

"Oh, that is totally fucked," she said bluntly, "And I'm quite happy to say so actually."

Kaben chuckled.

I ignored both of them and started looking for the gap that held the entrance. Behind me Alice said quietly to her mutt, "Nothing's changed. No conversation and straight for entry."

I ran my hands over the wall, working my fingertips into the grooves between each brick. There was a gap between two buildings that had been filled with sealant but nothing happened when I pressed against it. I walked several paces up the hill, towards the Norwich Castle, feeling the wall as I did with both my hands. I explored every detail, every imperfection, every little hole.

"Having trouble finding the spot?" Alice asked sweetly.

"You do know that you've been in Wonderland before as well?" I reminded her, "You could help."

"And miss the opportunity to see the great Donnie Rust in action?" she teased.

"Very funny. Is it true that you don't remember your time in there?"

"I remember bits and bobs," she said, "But none of it matches what that drug addict Carroll wrote about. My memories of the place are more fragmented and detached. I was there. I was young. Can you remember everything of your childhood?"

"I can scarcely remember last week." I remarked, "Aha!"

I found the gap I was looking for and the wall snapped open to reveal a short alleyway of ten feet leading to a very simple, quite boring wooden door. Someone had hammered in several wooden boards across it.

"Your handiwork?" Alice enquired.

"I guess so," I stepped into the alleyway and with my hands in my pockets, bent double and took a closer look at the door, "There is no handle."

"You really didn't want anyone to go back in, did you?"

"Least of all me."

"Are you having second thoughts?"

"Oh! I'm long passed those my dear," I said, "But a deal is a deal."

"And what is the deal?"

I pried the boards away from the door and stacked them along the side wall of the alleyway. I ran my hand cautiously across the door's surface.

"Well?" Alice persisted.

"I'll tell you in a bit, for now we have bigger problems like this door. It isn't going to open for us."

"Alice had no problem getting into her rabbit hole." Kaben observed.

"Me neither."

There was another yank of the chain and I heard Alice grunt a little under the effort.

Placing my hands against the door, I found it firmly and solidly shut. Not like the doors of today which are always so breakable, this was solid oak with iron couplings and heavy hinges attached to stone. It was a door that preferred being closed.

"So why are you doing this?" Alice persisted.

I gave up, stepping away from the door and scratching my head, "I was doing it to save a monster, but that won't matter if I can't get you inside."

"Saving a monster? That doesn't sound like you." She said, bluntly.

"I won't rise to that, Alice," I pointed out. Then turning my attention to her looming comrade, I said, "Kaben, looks like you are up! Reckon you can take down this door?"

The street lamps cast a golden light upon Kaben's bristly grey-brown fur as he stood at the entrance to the alleyway. His boulder-like shoulders rose almost to the height of his pointy ears. Some of his fur bristled and his yellow eyes narrowed at me. He turned his long, lupine head to Alice and said, "May I, mistress?"

The bounty hunter shrugged and dropped the length of his chains from her sleeve to the paving stones where they coiled up in a great heap.

This pleased the wolf who grinned widely and without any hesitation ran at the door. It was impressive how much speed he gathered in the short distance and he struck it with the force of a tank rolling down a steep hill. There was a dull thump and a groan.

"Yeah, you're right it doesn't sound like me." I commented with a shrug, "But you know, some monsters need saving. Oh, look at this."

I pulled out a brass doorknob from my pocket and showed it to Alice, "I totally forgot about this."

Kaben got hurriedly to his feet and glowered at me, in a harsh whisper he said, "I am going to bite you little man."

"You'd better ask your mistress first," I said quietly to him.

"She doesn't like you any more than I do."

I smiled as sweetly as I was able, "Oh no Kaben, you don't like me, she hates me. You see I only tricked you. Now, please step aside, thank you."

With a throaty growl the wolf stepped to the side of the alleyway, far enough to get out of the way but not far enough that his hot breath didn't flutter the hairs at my neck.

I pressed the doorknob against the appropriate part of the door. There was a whirl of movement inside the doorknob as it sought out its old mechanisms.

From inside the door there were hundreds of answering clicks and clacks of movement.

"When the world is finally destroyed. Gods and aliens will be left looking at this door and wondering where it goes." I said, "It is one of those stubborn things that won't let you in unless you know how to ask."

The door clicked open.

"It just occurred to me, Alice that I haven't asked why you wanted to come to Wonderland." I said, "I told you my reason. What's your deal?"

Alice stepped passed me and put a gloved hand to the door, with the other she patted my cheek and said, "Oh don't worry, you're going to love this."

Kaben followed her, ducking double to get through the door. For a moment they were on one side of the door and I was on the other. I thought about closing it behind them and locking them in. Going home and having a rum. I was still thinking this as I stepped inside and closed the door behind me.

Inside the absolute blackness I was aware that I was in very close proximity of a wolf's rump.

"Where are we little man?" Kaben growled.

I tried to get around him but there wasn't the space, on either side of me there were obstructions that I tried to feel with my hands. Kaben mewed in the darkness, "Little man! Where are we?"

Kaben's afraid of the dark, the voice in my head said. It had taken a while, but the voice was back. That little beast we all have in the back of our heads. *Don't worry, I'll remember that little tidbit of information for you.*

"Alice, calm your hound," I muffled. My hands thudded against something that fell over with a clutter. My fingers passed over what felt like folded towels.

"We're in a closet." I said, "Alice can you find a door or a switch?"

"Hang on," Alice said, just a disembodied voice in my world of blackness and doghair. How could an animal shed so much hair and not be bald as an egg?

"Take your time." I wheezed.

"I'm looking for the switch," she said, "It has to be here somewhere. Where was it last time you were here?"

"Last time I was here? Last time I was here I was blind drunk. It should be on the wall or maybe hanging from a dangly string?"

There was a click and the room was filled with light. We were indeed in a linen closet, surrounded on both sides by folded towels and sheets and bleach which I had just knocked over.

I squeezed around Kaben and passed Alice and put my knob against the inside of the closet door. As the knob did its thing I said, "You should consider Alice, that as a child you were smart enough to forget this place. It drove Carroll crazy."

"And you?" she asked.

I gave her what I hoped was a significant look and pulled the door wide, "Welcome to Wonderland."

5.

"Where are we?" Alice asked.

We were standing in a corridor. Carpeted with a style of red diamonds on white. All along the high ceiling hung dusty, cobwebbed chandeliers. Along the walls right down to the far end where the corridor met a T-junction were doors with stylized numbers on them. A tune was playing, a crackly melody belonging to a funfair that promised further creepiness.

Alice rounded on me, "Where are we?"

"This is a hotel, you silly girl," I said, running my fingertips along the wall. They left trails in the dust that had collected there, two white streaks in a greying surface. I wiped the dust off with a handkerchief, "We are in a hotel in Wonderland."

"There are hotels in Wonderland?" She asked.

"Every land has its tourist industry," I said.

Kaben growled, "Watch your tone little man."

I sagged against the wall in exasperation, "Oh, wouldn't it just be easier to bark at me? Look, this is a hotel, Wonderland is a big place filled with many, many interesting people; they need a place a stay. Hence a hotel, although it would appear that the tourism industry is not exactly thriving…"

The door to the linen closet slammed shut. Alice tore it open and was presented with shelves of linen and rows of toilet bleach. No door with which to exit.

I slipped the doorknob back into my pocket and said, "So, we're not leaving that way. You're stuck with me now so why not tell me why we're here?"

Alice and Kaben exchanged a glance. He shrugged nonchalantly. She said, "We are here to collect a bounty on the one known as the Rabbit."

"Who is that?"

Alice shrugged and poked at the wall paper with a finger, "Also known as the White Rabbit. He is someone in the employ slash slavery of the Queen…"

"That doesn't seem like a lot to go on," I said, "You must know more."

"You ask a lot of questions little man," Kaben growled.

"That was three questions. That's not a lot. Or, is that as high as you're able to count?"

I think I saw his eyes go red for a second, but I walked away from him. He snarled fitfully at my back as I walked down the corridor, trying the doors as I went.

All of the doors opened into identical rooms. All of them with the same lay out of a queen-sized bed in a room, en-suite and diamond motif duvets and bedspreads. In one of them I went to the window and drew the curtains open.

"Hey, Alice, come have a look at your Wonderland."

"Oh, my goodness!" she gasped.

"Not what you remember?" I asked.

"Not really, I remember there being a sky for one thing."

I looked upwards. The sky was not blue, nor was it, technically sky. It looked like we were in a snow globe that had been dropped into a bucket of sludge. Or that space outside the world had congealed and curdled and now dark purple muck oozed above us occasionally revealing veins of phosphorous green. At ground level beyond the window were vast woods, foaming with vegetation cast into an upward light by glowing balls that apparently marked the roads. In the far distance was a castle and, in this castle, there were a lot more lights that showed surrounding that castle, not much grew.

Behind us someone cleared their throat politely.
Kaben, given too much free chain by Alice attacked the new arrival with a snarl but the wolf, despite his size was promptly thrown head first into the wall of the room. He staggered to his feet and persisted with an attack and once again was hurled head over heels with what was one of the smoothest aikido throws, I had ever witnessed. Almost two hundred kilograms of flying wolf smashed into the bed at high velocity and splintered it. The thrower resumed a position of humble servitude with his hands pressed together. He was very neat and gave an appropriate bow and introduced himself:

"My name is Harold and I am the hotel manager," he said, "I saw you three on the surveillance and wished to welcome you to Wonderland."
Kaben rolled off the bed with a groan.

"Hello Harold," Alice said, "Are all the hotel managers here so skilled?"

"Only the alive ones," he answered politely, "May I ask why you are in here? This is not your room."

"That could be difficult to explain," I said, stepping forward from the window, "So I won't try. But would it be possible for us to have a couple of rooms for the night?"

"Two nights," Alice opted in.

"Two nights," I echoed.

"At least." She added.

"At least." I echoed.

Harold, who was only about four feet tall and quite skinny save for his oversized hands and exceptionally straight back cast his small-eyed gaze across each of us in turn before saying, "Yes, I do have some rooms. Will we be needing three?"

"Two," Alice said, "Kaben stays with me."

Harold looked at me with a smile, "Mr Kaben is it?"

"I am Kaben!" Kaben growled sweeping away part of the bed with the back of his hand and standing. The little manager looked up at the wolf with a dulled interest.

"That is fine." He said, taking out a note book, "In that case, may I take your names please?"

We gave them to him. When I told him mine, he promptly closed his book and slipped it into his pocket and his smile lingered slightly longer than was pleasant.

Alice was asked to politely leave and Kaben followed her fairly meekly out of the hotel. I, on the other hand, was escorted out of the building by security who took great delight in tossing me through the front doors. Harold, who had been shouting continuously for the entire expedition down the stairs tossed a roll of paper at me that bounced on the ground at my feet.

"That is for you." He hissed at me, "And it is due!"

He pointed a threatening finger at me and stalked up the stairs into the hotel. I brushed off my jacket and looked up at the building. It was a refurbished castle, old and gothic, severely gnarly with gargoyles and twisted metal spires. I pinched the skin between my eyes and moaned as a few recollections managed to surface from the deeper pits of memory.

"He gives us toilet paper for the journey?" Kaben asked, picking up the roll of paper.

"It's not toilet paper," I said.

"What is it?" Alice asked.

"My bill." I said.

We took to the road that led in the direction of the giant castle which was where we assumed the Queen would be. The road was made up of irregular paving stones, all jutting out at awkward angles as if they had warped in great heat or been disheveled by a great earthquake. Meanwhile, the canopy of trees was thick like a thatched roof and the only light we had came from giant glowing mushrooms along the side of the road.

We were walking for no more than ten minutes when Kaben went mental. Growling and snapping at something ahead of us in the lane, tugging hard on the chain and clawing at the paving slabs; it was as if he had seen a cat.

As it was, he had.

"Hey Donnie," she said seductively as she walked three feet above the stones towards us,

twirling her tail in slow circles as if it were a pocket watch, "Fancy seeing you here."
Alice rocked slightly as Kaben tugged on the chain, grunting, "Oh, of course, you would know this … thing?"

"Hi, Cheshire," I said, "How are you?"

"I'm okay," the cat said to me, purring, "I should be angry with you. You did say that you would come right back. I don't know if you lied or were just detained. So, I can't really be angry with you, so I'm not. I am glad to see you though perhaps we could continue where we left off?"

Alice cleared her throat and suddenly sounded very put-off, "Are you not going to introduce us Donnie?"

"Sorry," I said, "Cheshire, this is Alice, Alice this is Cheshire. Cheshire, this is her dog. Yes Alice, I have had sex with Cheshire and yes, Cheshire I have had sex with Alice. You were both very good but not good enough for me to want to compare. Kaben sit down."
The wolf was staring fixatedly at Cheshire, his ass plonked onto the paving slabs with a thump.

"Your dog likes me," she said, tipping her top hat and blowing him a kiss.
Kaben didn't even respond. His eyes were a little blank. I could understand Cheshire was probably flicking a few of his triggers. It was actually a little disconcerting to see.

"We should be getting on," I prompted but Cheshire blocked the lane. She adjusted the lapels of her fine, purple coat with the silver embroidery, which if memory served, I stole from one of Wonderland's pirates last time I was here. Beneath the coat she wore a black lace corset and a thick collared white shirt with puffy sleeves. The corset really did hug her fine curves and matched the coy bowler hat she wore quite finely.

"But I haven't seen you in an age," she whined, walking up to me and batting her eyelids.

"No time," I said, "Sorry. Hey! Get your tail out of there!"

Cheshire skipped back girlishly, each step taking her a foot higher into the air where she hovered, wagging her bum, "Oh? You didn't complain last time?"

"Are you blushing?" Kaben asked.

"Shut up," I grunted, then to Alice I said, "Let's carry on."

"No, hold on," Alice said, pinching her chin in thought, "I think that this little introduction into your past could warrant some attention."

I groaned loudly.

"Miss," Alice said stepping forward, "I take it you are the Cheshire Cat from legend?"

Cheshire looked down at Alice as if seeing her for the first time. Like Kaben, Cheshire appeared mostly human, where it counted, save for the furry paws, retractable claws, tail and the ears. There was also this thing she did when she – you know what? Never mind, I'm not telling you.

"Oh, my goodness," Cheshire exclaimed, "You're Alice!"

"Yes," Alice confirmed.

"*The* Alice?" Cheshire asked, putting her hands together and descending solemnly to the paving stones, "Do you not remember me?"

"It has been a long time since I came here," Alice said, "Regrettably, I don't remember much at all about it."

"Oh," Cheshire said, with what I was starting to suspect was mock feeling, "Well that is a shame. We were so enamoured by your visit that when dear Mr. Carroll visited, we told him all about you and your little adventure here."

"She has played a part in many stories," Kaben grumbled.

"So sorry Cheshire," I perked up, "I forgot this is the Big Bad Wolf. Do you know the tail of Little Red Riding Hood?"

Cheshire put her head to the side, her yellow eyes blinking merrily, "Oh my Alice, you do get around."

"Can you tell us if the Queen at the castle?"

"I certainly can tell you," Cheshire said with a smile.

"Well?" Alice prompted.

"Well what?"

"Cheshire," I said, folding my arms, "Please…"

"You can only ever expect the answer to the question," the cat pointed out and slowly rotated around on the point so that her upside down head was now six feet in the air and her feet were pressed against an imaginary ceiling above, "Ask the right question and you will no doubt receive the right answer."

"Is the Queen at the castle?" Alice asked, pointing in the direction of the castle we were heading towards.

"A queen will almost certainly be in a castle," Cheshire confirmed, folding her arms and looking thoughtful, "Or else there will be an empty chair and a lonely king don't you think? Assuming that things are still classical?"

"The Queen, the Queen of Wonderland," Alice said, "Is she at that castle."

The cat purred thoughtfully, I had felt the effect of that purring and tried to keep a straight face.

"Depends on your allegiance really, doesn't it?" Cheshire asked, "Also, weren't you blonde last time you came here?"

Alice's cheeks flushed red with frustration.

"Will you please take us to the Queen of Hats?" I asked finally, abandoning pretense.

Cheshire continued the rotation, spinning slowly on her axis until her high heeled boot ends reached the paving stones.

"That is why I was sent," she said, "So I see no issue in doing it. Please follow me."

She started walking in front of us and as she did, she looked at Kaben over her shoulder and went, "Woof."

I caught Alice as she was yanked off her feet this time.

"Who is the Queen of Hats?" Alice asked as we followed Cheshire, "I thought this place was ruled over by the Red and White Queens? I think I remember something about a chess board and cards?"

"Oh, it used to be," Cheshire said, suddenly appearing between us, Kaben whined angrily and she stuck out her tongue. Her slightly rough tongue, like wet sand paper... anyway, she ignored my warning glance and said, "It was all like that until Donnie visited us."

Alice shot me a glance, "What the hell did you do with my Wonderland?"

"Nothing," I said quickly.

"Oh, hardly nothing," Cheshire teased merrily, rising up over us both in a painfully slow somersault, as if she swam through the air. She ended up leaning backwards at an angle as if resting against an invisible wall that was moving behind so that she drifted in front of us, "Shall I tell you the story?"

"No." I said.

"Yes please," Alice said.

Cheshire sighed, "So, everything was hunky dory after dear Mr. Carroll spent some time here and then went off to write his little book- is it doing well by the way?"

"It's doing okay," I said.

"Good for him," she said with a happy grin, "He was such a nice man. Unfortunately, bad breath but you know?" she said looking up at the canopy and stroking her chin, "Of repugnant qualities his was not that bad. And we generally are quite used to eccentrics in Wonderland."

"Then Donnie visited?" Alice prompted.

"Well, we always have visitors to Wonderland," Cheshire said conversationally, "You know, they fall in quite frequently but usually assume it is a dream. Like many tourists, they wander around for a bit, observe a lot of things, embarrass themselves and leave."

"Then Donnie visited?" Alice said again.

"Indeed," Cheshire said giving me a beaming smile, "I have never seen a man more inebriated. It usually takes a certain kind of mind to fall into Wonderland, narcotics are pretty good at doing it, changes the brain in just the right way to open a door. But this man managed it on alcohol alone. I've always wanted to know; how much exactly did you drink that night?"

I was not participating in the conversation and chose to say nothing.

"My point," Cheshire said happily, "So! He arrives. Long story short he roofied the tea party so that the Mad Hatter and the March Hare ended up doing it in the windmill, then they wrapped the field mouse in cellophane and shoved it right up the Mad Hatter's..."

Through the twisted trunks of the woods, that brought new definitions to words like "gnarled", "inhospitable" and "dark" there came an ear shredding wail. As mechanical as it was organic it brought gooseflesh across my arms. It made Kaben's hackles go on end and Alice spun to face it. When it ended, we all exchanged a worried glance.

"What the hell was that?" Alice asked me.

"I have no idea. Chesh?"

But she hadn't stopped talking.

"- he was then taken to the Red Queen who, as everyone knows, has a bit of a thing for the grotesque and he showed her his, you know what, and she was instantly enamoured. Poor woman. Then at a massive feast in his honour he literally drinks everyone under the table and takes the Red Queen over her own throne while spanking her with one of her flamingo pogo sticks, right before he shoved it up her..."

"Excuse me, what was that noise?" Alice asked.

"Oh, that's just Benny," Cheshire said off handed, "*Then,* he manages to find his way into the Dodos apothecary and spikes the water supply of the queendom with narcotic aphrodisiacs. He then did me from behind on the Red Queen's chopping board. We got caught though!"

"You vanished," I said.

"It's instinct," Cheshire said, "Anyway, he ended up naked and, in the stocks, and the Red Queen's army took turns to…"

"Who is Benny?" Alice pressed.

"No, what did the army do?" Kaben asked.

"The Caterpillar," I coughed into my fist.

"The Caterpillar's name is Benny?"

Cheshire shrugged, "Oh yes, the Caterpillar that was so wise and smart when you came here first Alice. He had a proper chinwag with you while he was taking his morning medicinal. Thought you were ever so clever and you got on so well because he was so wise."

"Then Donnie visited?" all three of us said at the same time.

After Cheshire finished the story, we had walked quite a distance into the woods. Behind us the path twisted itself into the woodland like a ball of string knotting itself and ahead of us it curved majestically like a river, with giant glowing mushrooms along its edges. Overhead occasionally the canopy of tree branches broke long enough to reveal the soupy texture of the sky.

"So," Alice said to me, "You accidentally came here and drank Wonderland to its knees?"

"I respect that," Kaben said.

"If he hadn't been so inebriated, we would have thought it was a declaration of war from the outside world. But as bombed as he was, it was like watching dominos fall. He ran away however when the Hat took over."

"The Hat?"

"I did not run away," I argued sharply, "I was asked politely to leave."

"And given a special key that would always allow you back in," Cheshire said, "You could have checked in to see how things were. To see how we were. See how I was."

"What did the Hat do?" Alice asked.

"Afterwards, the kingdom was devastated, lost. The hangover we felt as a land was apocalyptic. The Hat's former owner was forced to face what he had done to his friends and committed suicide the only way he knew how. He blew a raspberry at the Red Queen who immediately had him beheaded. The executioner, who Donnie had challenged to a game of one for one the night before, only did the job half well. The Mad Hatter, what was left of him, fled to the White Queen who, upon seeing him and, with a cluster headache immediately abandoned the pretence of being a "good queen", declared war."

Kaben's chops drew back in a big grin, "I *like* this story," he said. Meanwhile, I could feel the icy air around Alice next to me.

"What happened then?" she asked.

"War, all-out war," Cheshire said now speaking solely to Alice, "But the armies were in no shape for it. The cards of the Red Queen stayed in their decks and refused to come out - so, with a temper already short at the best of times - she had them all executed. The White Queen's forces arrived upon the castle to see the Red Queen executing all of her soldiers. As all of her army were already very, *very* tired and headachy they set to work killing whatever soldiers were standing and in the confusion many of the front line turned on the line behind them due to lack of numbers and started fighting. The Bandersnatch, the Jabberwocky and the Jubjub bird were summoned."

""Beware the Jabberwocky, my son! The jaws that bite, the claws that catch! Beware the Jubjub bird, and shun the frumious Bandersnatch!" Kaben said.
All of us stopped walking and turned to stare.

"What?" he said, "I read."

"Anyway," Cheshire said, "*Donnie* here had visited them as well during his little drinking mission and introduced them to kamikaze tequilas. So, when these three arrived the Bandersnatch was nearly blind, the JubJub bird couldn't fly straight and the Jabberwocky vomited on its own claws and slipped on the stairs."

"Did they fight?" Kaben asked.

"They destroyed the army pretty well," Cheshire said, "But it wasn't much of a fight."

"What about the Vorpal sword?" Kaben asked, "Did it go *snicker-snack?*"

"Oh, the *Vorpal* sword," Cheshire said, turning her head and giving me a very severe cat-like look, "Do you want to share with the class what you did with the Vorpal sword?"

I didn't look up from my shoes but shook my head.

"Let's just say that the Vorpal sword was not available," Cheshire said, "So, those three destroyed the armies of both red and white. The Queen's sisters were so destressed that they took a nap and during this nap the Hat, now, no longer attached to the Mad Hatter's head, took its chance and found a new owner. And what you see now is the result."

"I didn't know," I said.

"Of course not," Cheshire said, "You left and didn't come back to find out what you'd done."

My shoulders sagged about seven inches and I took a cold, unhappy breath. Alice and Cheshire walked ahead, Kaben on the other hand, came up to me and put a giant paw on my shoulder.

"I respect that level of tomfuckery," he said with a grin, "You and I are friends."

Alice yanked on his chain and he winked at me and lumbered to catch up with her.

"Perfect." I whispered.

6.

With the castle still a fair distance away we entered into a clearing near a slow-moving river. In the clearing there was a long wooden table. Tall weeds grew up through gaps in the wood, obscuring the broken saucers, tea pots and cups. Around the table were upturned chairs, so wrapped up in ivy it looked like the grass was slowly ingesting them. At the head of the table sat a scruffy grey furred hare in a waistcoat.

We paused to watch him for a moment, because his presence begged several questions. Namely, if there were no whole cups on the table, why was he so fuzzy around the edges, as if he survived on a diet of pure caffeine? This was answered when, without blinking his eyes he brought up a quivering hand armed with a steel syringe and without so much as a flinch plunged it directly into his neck and depressed the stopper.

"Holy shit!" I cried.

"There is nothing holy about this place anymore," Cheshire said then in a merry voice she called out, "Oh, Hare! Oh, Hare are you here?"

She floated across the grass towards the poor creature that now had both hands firmly fixed on the edge of the table and was making the broken fragments of the crockery rattle.

As Cheshire approached the waistcoat-wearing hare tore his gaze away from the space directly in front of him and rolled his bloodshot eyes to her.

"Oh," he jittered, "Hello Cheshire.... It's been at least five minutes since you were here. At least. Possibly more. But definitely at least 5 minutes. I'm sure of it. How are you?"

"I am good my lovely," Cheshire said, bowing at the waist and looking for a second that she was being suspended by her tail, "Look, I have brought some of my friends for tea."

With eyes that were so dry that they scraped when they moved, the hare looked at us. He didn't look at our faces but glared at our feet.

"They're on my grass!" he shrieked, suddenly springing up and running across the table, smashing crockery with his mangy feet and swinging a kettle handle above his head, "Get off my grass! Get off my grass! Get off my grass!"

In unison the three of us leapt back onto the lane and the instant we landed on the lane the hare relaxed, completely. He toppled forward, bounced face first off the long table and landed with an anorexic thump upon the grass which he hugged fiercely.

"Oh, my lovely, lovely grass!" he cried, burying his face into it.

Cheshire floated over to us, casting a worried look back at the hare.

"I should have mentioned. He is a little precious about his grass. You need to walk on the stepping stones," she said, gesturing with a sweep of her tail to a line of raised blocks that ran from the lane to the table.

None of us moved at first, but I could feel that the expectation was on me.

"Fine," I said, "I'll go first."

I stepped from the lane onto the first raised bock and the second I did the hare's face shot up out of the grass with his long ears as rigid as planks. His unnerving eyes wide and bulging. But once he realized I was on the stepping stone and not the grass he sighed and rolled onto his back.

"In days of old when knights were bold," he chanted, "And paper had not been invented. We wiped our ass with a blade of grass and then he was contented!"

"This rabbit is off his rocker," Alice said.

The hare rocketed from where he lay and landed on the table, "Rabbit?! I am not The Rabbit; I am the Hare! The March Hare do you hear? Don't you ever, *ever* refer to me as a rabbit or things will get really hairy for you!"

"She apologizes," I said, which instantly placated the hare who flopped upon the table.

"A table is a lark m'lord, a table is a tree, not a throne or a stool my lord, but somewhere you drink your tea." He chanted happily.

I looked back at Alice and mouthed, *What is in that coffee?*

Cheshire had floated to the head of the table where the hare had originally been sitting and, while the hare continued muttering poetry to himself, we used the stepping stones to join her.

"Why have we stopped here?" I asked, "I think we would all like to reach the Queen of Hats sooner rather than later."

Cheshire smiled and inclined her top hat mockingly, "Just say the word Donnie, you *know* how much I love being told what to do."

"I would like to know why we're here as well," Alice said on the stepping stone behind me. Kaben was spinning his arms trying to stay on the stone immediately behind her.

"Hare is an old friend," Cheshire said, "I haven't seen him in over five minutes, and I wanted to make sure he is okay and to restock his supply."

She took from the interior pocket of her long coat a vial of dark brown liquid and picked up the syringe that the hare, named Hare, had used. She jabbed the needle through the top and withdrew the stopper, sucking all the thick liquid out.

"One hundred percent pure Wonderland coffee," she explained, "He used to drink tea, bless his heart, but he's all alone now and he doesn't like the taste of coffee. So, a needle it is."

I looked over to the hare, he was now sat upright, his big feet out in front of him on the table, his potato chip nailed toes wriggling as he swayed backwards and forwards, his ears jerking erratically.

It wasn't said but it was clear that this was my fault as well. I looked away from the scene with distaste and stared at the line of trees near where the river joined the clearing. Mushrooms illuminated the darkness softly.

I recalled snippets of the part of my party in Wonderland that included The Mad Hatter, the March Hare and the field mouse. Saluting each other with tea cups brimming with dark spirit, declaring our devotion to each other and our abandonment of our limitations, which resulted in The Mad Hatter pulling out a roll of cellophane and saying he had something he wanted to try.

The next images available in my mind involved me supporting myself against the windmill's wall, as the Mad Hatter promised the Field Mouse he knew what he was doing while wrapping the small creature in cellophane while The March Hare giggled like a maniac.

Looking up the river I saw the remains of that windmill, brought down to its foundations and now just a circle of stones in the grass.

You're the one who drove the Mad Hatter to commit suicide, that voice in my head said to me.

The air was humid and smelt rancid like the river, I rubbed at my neck and took a breath. I felt dirty in my shirt and tie, out of place in my usually comfortable black suit. Usually my suit was my armour, but now it felt like it belonged on someone else. I also wanted a shower and a long kip.

"Oh Alice," Hare said wistfully, pulling me back to the present, "I remember when you were here last time. I can remember that. You were such a preciously innocent creature, in blue dresses and white petticoats."

"I wish I could remember you better Mister March Hare," Alice said politely.

With a creaking of dehydrated muscles and tendons the hare turned his head beyond the line of his waist-

coated shoulder and peered at her with unblinking eyes, "You were so pretty... and so willing to please."
I really didn't like the unnerving monotomaticism that his voice had taken on. Even less as he continued.
"You wanted so much for us to invite you to tea." He said, "You did whatever the Hatter asked of you. You were such a good, little girl for him. But not for me..."
It happened in slow motion.
Hare's face didn't move a muscle until he was already flinging himself at Alice, his claws ripping out splinters from the table as he tore across it. Ears flat against his head, his lips drawn back revealing long terrifying incisors like yellow chisels, and a waist coat with all the buttons buttoned – he looked like something catapulted out of a nightmare.

Kaben was off-balance and saw what was happening too late. Alice's hands were rising to protect her face which was whitened with an unusual expression of scant surprise. Cheshire was still pulling at the plunger, her tongue stuck out in the effort to get the last of the coffee from the vial.
The heel of my shoe connected with the March Hare's bony jaw just beneath his bulging eyes and with all the force I could put into the kick. The sideward angle of it pitched both me and the hare away from the stepping stones. I skidded on the grass top, tearing up tufts of it while he rolled across it with all the drama of a football player. He was up on his feet in an instant.

"My grass! My grass! Get off my grass!" he shrieked maddeningly as he charged at me at all fours, leaping to slash at my face.

He was skinny, mostly comprised of fur and bone held together with tendons and when I round house kicked him it was like kicking a wicker basket. Spurred on by caffeine in its purest, brown form he bounced off the table and tried to bite at my face with his malicious fangs. I brought my elbow up in reflex and the tip of it cleanly struck with his chin. An enamel yellowed incisor broke with a metallic clink and went sailing up into the gloom.

It was all going so well right before he struck me with both hind legs right in the fork.

The sudden mind blanking pain shot up from my crotch and I staggered. He kicked me twice, each time felt like being hit by a bamboo sham bock. With one hand clutching my crotch, the other managed to shield the blows but one of them connected hard with my cheek bone.

I rode the force of the kick and rolled across the grass, coming to a crouch some distance away. The hare shrieked with inconsolable rage and flew at me again, his arms flapping around.

"Feel free to join in if you like?" I shouted at the rest of the group but didn't have time to see what they were doing because I was dealing with a storm of furry kicks and bloody teeth trying to rip the skin off my skull.

Nails slashed deep gouges across my face and my chest and I was driven backwards away from the table into the darker parts of the field near the sluggish water where the glowing mushrooms did not glow.

"Get off my grass!" he shrieked again, his next scream being one of such a high insanity that it didn't just hurt my ears but made my teeth shiver. I was recoiling from this sound when I spotted something more horrifying between his legs and as he threw what would be his final kick, I acted without thinking.

I ducked, reached up without looking, found the one thing I was most desperate to avoid touching and grabbed it in my fist.

Sparing too many details, were you aware that like all leporids, hares have a baculum? And have you ever broken off a dried stick from a tree branch? Yes. You get the idea. It cracked.

His enraged howling abruptly stopped.

If you were out of earshot you might have thought that he was still screaming at me. It looked like it, his mouth was wide, the cheeks stretched, his bulging eyes bulged as if they were going to pop right out of his face. The only difference from before was that his left bottom eyelid twitched and the sound he was making was the high-pitched, gassy squeal of someone too scared to breathe.

It didn't last. He was soon screaming again but it was an entirely different pitch and it was from the ground where he had curled into a tight, shivering ball.

I ran around in a circle, wiping my hand frantically on my trouser leg and making ridiculous sounds of disgust. Furiously I stamped across the grass to the table, digging my heels in on each step to tear up the roots while shouting.

"If you'd have helped me out, I wouldn't have needed to do that to his- oh...hell."

It was quickly evident that I had been had as a fool.

Cheshire was perched upon the back of the March Hare's chair, her legs crossed, head resting on her shoulder and a whimsical smile on her face. Meanwhile, Alice and Kaben were sat at the table, wrapped up in a pair of tree trunks. Kaben's shoulders bulged as he strained to get free, but Alice appeared to be unconscious, her head slumped to the side.

"Cheshire," I said as I neared, "What is going on here?"

The cat's tail danced in the air and her grin widened, but not from what I had said but from the sound of the March Hare's horrific screams. It was, by several degrees, worse to witness.

"You have no idea the sorts of things that the March Hare is guilty of," she said, "After all the screams he has caused he makes such lovely music, doesn't he?"

"Why are my friends tied up?" I asked.

"I mean," she said, "I had expected you to break his neck... I hadn't even considered breaking his..."

"Cheshire!" I said loudly, "Why are my friends tied up?"

"Do his screams disturb you?" she asked, looking at me directly.

I didn't answer, but I knew I wouldn't be able to put a hand to myself again without thinking of *snap.* With a *poof!* Cheshire vanished from the chair top and reappeared crouched in front of the Marching Hare. The poor creature looked up at her and whimpered, "He b-b-b-b-broke me."

What she did next made my skin curl and even stopped Kaben from struggling. She reached down between the hare's legs and the screams that followed lifted birds from the surrounding trees, he kicked out his arms and legs and tried to bat her away while her eyes widened over her smile.

I turned my back to them and ran to where Alice and Kaben were bound and on this side of the table I could see that she wasn't held by tree trunks at all.

Hare's screams stopped suddenly and in a cloud of purple smoke Cheshire appeared perched on the side of the table between Alice and Kaben, her legs crossed.

"Going somewhere Donnie?" she asked.

From either side of me two blades, each seven feet in length, cut out of the ground like closing scissors and as fast as my reactions were, it was more luck than anything that saved me from being cleanly cut in two. What I had thought was a Wonderland equivalent of a bear trap turned out to be something far more monstrous as the ground underneath me suddenly ruptured.

I sprawled on the dirt and stared up with wide-eyed terror as the monster kept coming out of the ground.

A long body, made of hundreds of segmented armoured joints, each with a pair of boney spikes sticking out of the sides as legs, ended on one side with a fairly plutonic tail that had wrapped around Kaben and Alice but on the other side was a head dominated by gigantic blade-like mandibles and a face of wriggling tentacles.

It arched its body at the height of a two-storied building and looked down at me.

"You remember Benny?" Cheshire asked, inspecting her claws.

"That's Benny?" I shrieked, backpedaling away from the monster, "What the fuck happened to him?"

"Oh, you know, The Hat has changed us all." she said.

Benny's body heaved and two streams of white snotty silk hit the earth where I had been, dissolving it right down to the bedrock. I was on my feet by this stage and running towards the trees as fast as I could.

"Benny!" Cheshire shouted, "You know Queenie wants him in one piece!"

The Caterpillar gave that same metallic/organic scream we had heard earlier and crashed to the ground, rattling the world as it burrowed under the earth to pursue me. I changed my direction, turning back on myself and sprinting for the table over what I imagined was Benny's back as he tore through the ground beneath my feet.

My gambit worked because he surfaced at the point behind me where I had turned and had to pull backwards through the earth, dirt and Hare's beloved grass to catch up with me.

Cheshire looked up from her claws with mild interest and her eyes widened with surprise as I dove between Kaben and Alice and tackled her around her waist.

She squeaked as both of us clattered over the table top and fell onto the other side where I pinned her to the floor, hands holding her wrists down, my bodyweight keeping her body flat.

"Gotcha!" I said.

Cheshire didn't struggle, she just drew her lips back away from her sharp teeth and licked them, "Oh, you poor man," she crooned, "Whose got who?"

From behind me her tail whipped around my throat and dragged me back. I tried to fight it but it had me at a disadvantage and before I knew it, I was on my back and Cheshire had me sat on the floor with her thighs wrapped around my waist.

"Well Cheshire, now this is familiar," I wheezed, "So happy to have common ground!"

She was panting through a smile, her hackles up. I had seen that look before in her eyes but doubted things were going to go the same way as they had then.

"Benny," she said, "Take those two to the castle, I will meet you there with this one."

The Caterpillar hissed and started away. I couldn't see where it went but I heard trees crashing as it moved through the forest.

"So, you want to finish off where we were?" I croaked.

Her eyes were right in front of mine and seemed uncertain for a second, it was a brief expression. Probably stemming from the point that any human would have been unconscious by now, the strength of her thighs was crushing my insides to mulch and her tail had cut off all air to my brain. But I was not, in most respects, human anymore.

"You were holding out on me," she said, "I never knew you were this resilient."

"You never tried to kill me before," I reminded her.

"Such a shame, can you imagine what we could have done," she teased, then her eyes took on a darker shade and she said, "You left me here, Donnie. You promised you wouldn't leave me here and you left me here!"

Her tail tightened around my throat, it wasn't enough to kill me, but it hurt. She lost interest in it though and let me go, I fell backwards.

Cheshire stood and strode away, her shoes not even touching the grass, "I mean why would you make promises you didn't mean to keep?"

"I was drunk." I reminded her. Pushing myself up.

"So, because you were drunk you made a bunch of promises you had no intention of keeping?"

"No, I don't need to be drunk to do that."

She faced me and hugged herself. An expression of such shattering vulnerability that I prayed she was faking.

"I was the fool then to believe you."

"I'm sorry Chesh, but this is your home. Why would you want to leave it for me?"

She laughed at the sky, "Oh you poor little fool," she said, "I didn't want to go with you. I just wanted to get out of here. It was bad before you arrived and you left it even worse afterwards, so you can imagine my disdain."

"Can I really be blamed for all of this?" I asked hauling myself up with the help of the table, "It wasn't all my fault."

"I know that deep down you have a very low opinion of your abilities, but yes. Yes! All of this is your

fault. Even sober you speak like a true drunk," she muttered, "Assuming that everyone will forgive you because you're not the same man when you succumb to your vices. You're no better than the Hare!"
I looked over to where the animal was lying, curled up in a ball near the river's edge. He had passed out it seemed or died.

"What did he do to you?"
Cheshire floated back to the table and sat on it, primly crossing one of her legs over the other, "Nothing to me of course. But his appetites are unspeakable. The Mad Hatter was a pervert," she said wistfully, "But harmless ultimately. He was careful with whom he involved himself and invited to his little tea parties. He only started to slip up when the March Hare became involved with him."

"And that brings me to my next question, what did he do to Alice?"
She gave me a reproachful look, as if that question was actually painful for her to be asked. She said, "When she arrived at the tea party the first time it was that vile thing lying over there that took the lead."

"The lead?"

"He liked the innocent ones who didn't know better, he said he was introducing them to the real world," she said, "The Queens had laws about it, making something as sickening as that illegal and punishable by death was one of the only things those idiots could agree on. But, after you visited, these perverts were given much more freedom because there was nobody to enforce the laws. The Hare now likes to scare."

I listened, while Cheshire's eyes took on a vacant look as if she was seeing something I couldn't, "He likes to take children and frighten them, it delights him. Without the balancing influence of the Mad Hatter he has been free to expand his tastes and has become the equivalent of a boogey man in these parts. The Queen of Hats sends the children of her enemies to come stay with The March Hare."

The March Hare quivered and made a plaintive, mewling sound.

Cheshire hopped off the table, "We have some time before I have to deliver you to Queenie. Come with me, I want to show you something. Something that you help build."

She led me across the grass away from the tea party table and the lane towards the line of trees, speaking as she went, "Imagine being taken away from your parents and being told by the all-powerful Queen of Hats that instead of being punished you were being sent to enjoy a tea party with a talking hare." She shook her head, "It would break your heart to know how long that excitement stays on their faces."

7.

At the trees, I saw a path that had been trodden through into the dirt, it led into the darkness of the woods but was wide enough for a line of children to walk along. The glowing mushrooms, with their bright light only succeeded in stirring the darkness at the edges.

Cheshire beckoned me to follow her and floated along the path, I kept at her heels obediently, but felt leadened.

Mushrooms, glowing in blues, greens and purples climbed up the trunks of the many trees and illuminated our path giving us just enough light to see where the path was, but not enough for me to have any idea where it was leading.

Things moved in the forest, as they do, hidden beneath the shrouds of vegetation and shadow things crawled. Things slithered, bounced and galumphed.

"We didn't spend a lot of time talking when you were last here," Cheshire remarked, "I would like to know more about you."

"Why?" I asked candidly, "Is it important if you're just going to trade me off to your Queen?"

Turning in midair Cheshire gave me a hurt expression, "You make me sound like a traitor."

"Aren't you?"

"Well, no," she said, "I told you I was instructed to come and collect you. This is what I'm doing."

"And Benny?"

"The Queen grew impatient and sent her Caterpillar," Cheshire explained, "But that doesn't make me a traitor. Does this mean you are the sort of person who sees assassins and demons in every shadow?"

I chuckled, "A day in my shoes. If nothing else paranoia keeps you alive."

"That's true," she said, turning back to face the direction of the path. That she floated above it and didn't offer anything in the sound of footsteps was bothering me, it meant I was all too aware of the noise I was making as I stumbled and fell over exposed bedrock and tree roots. Black handmade Italian shoes were not made for the forest. Neither was my black, two-buttoned suit of imported silks. It seemed to attract twigs and leaves and hooked pieces of bark.

Cheshire stopped near the massive twisted trunk of a tree. Not just any tree. It was one of *those* trees. The sort of tree that only appears in German fairytales. Every forest has one. A tree that is so out of place that it looks as if some sort of monstrous evil must be imprisoned inside and corrupting it.

"There is a monstrous evil imprisoned in this tree," Cheshire said.

"He brought the children here?" I asked, keeping my distance from the corrupted trunk so that I could get a better look at it. It didn't look much in the way of a tree at all but rather like some kind of extreme slow-motion explosion of wood. The trunk bulged and twisted around itself for the height of fifteen feet before the gnarled and clawed branches erupted from the top reaching out here and there prepared to grab anything coming close enough and dragging it inside. It looked like the pride and joy of HP Lovecraft's hobby garden.

"Oh yes, it would help him separate the children who were brave from those who were easily scared," she said, "I used to watch."

"Watch? You never tried to stop it?"

"They were the Queen of Hats' enemies, weren't they?" she asked.

I folded my arms and looked at the tree for a while longer, "It's definitely a scary tree, but it's just a tree."

Not looking away from the rough, black bark she said, "He would dare the children to touch the tree. Naturally, the brave and unafraid would... those who were cowards would no- Don't touch it?!"

I withdrew my hand, "Why? It's just a tree."

Cheshire had both hands outreached, even her boots pointed in my direction as if she would grab me with every limb she had to pull me away. My fingertips were mere centimetres away from the bark. I waggled them mischievously and saw her tail twitch, "Just come here Donnie, I want to show you the rest of the trip

"You want to know some things about me Cheshire?" I said putting my hand on the bark, "Don't ever try to intimidate me because it won't work – "

The bark on the tree wasn't bark at all and during daylight this would have been blatantly obvious. Instead this whole tree was made up of hands. Clasping over each other, wooden and rotten but alive, these hands formed an armour around the tree's surface, holding in whatever monster was inside.

One of these hands snared my wrist.

"Cheshire!" I yipped, tugging at my arm as the hand held me firm. The first attempts to escape proved fruitless but the more I pulled and struggled the more give there seemed to be in the limb. But I couldn't break free.

"You're such an idiot - stop struggling!" Cheshire shouted in my ear.

"Sod that!" I shouted, grabbing my forearm with my other hand and digging my heels in as I tore myself away from the tree and took the hand with me. But the hand was attached to an arm, which was attached to a body, which had a head on it.

Like the wet sap on the inside of bark, the body was less wooden than the hand itself, raw even. I couldn't see many details of it other than it was greasy, it stank like rotten meat and there were no other limbs. Just a torso with one arm and a moaning head.

The body thudded hard against the ground, let go of my wrist and vanished into the shadows.

I recoiled, running backwards as fast as my legs could carry me shouting, "Cheshire! Cheshire where the hell are you!?"

The body from the tree was moving, propelled by the stumps of its legs and hauled forward by its one working arm. With a frantic mania, it moved like this at a terrifying speed. A weeping wound of a body, wet, moist, contaminated and furious and with a wet sucking sound, it scrambled over the dirt towards me.

I ran. My word did I run.

I had never felt fear like this. It was a childish fear. An instinctive terror, far more primal and deeper than any mere adult fright. The sort of fear that is branded upon our very bones the moment we slip out of our mothers. It was the fear of being chased in the dark by something diseased and wet.

Cheshire was nowhere to be seen. I was surrounded on all sides by darkness so absolute I thought I had gone blind and this thing, this broken, angry, wet thing was chasing me through the underbrush. Clawed fingers scratching at the back of my shoes.

Running, I tried to keep to the pathway, but the mushrooms were no longer lighting my path and I had to navigate by my shoes. Branches mockingly slapped me in the face and clawed at my shoulders, I stumbled and staggered as this thing grunted and yapped behind me, pursuing me relentlessly.

What would happen when it caught me? That's what drove me to flee, not the fear of pain, but the fear of not seeing this thing. That unknown element painted a picture in my mind of a monster that was little and evil. Like a young toddler running at you with a knife blade while laughing. You wouldn't kick it; you'd run and hide.

I had nowhere to hide. So, I ran.

And one thing anyone who has run through a forest at night will tell you: forests are not meant to be run through.

Firstly, the ground started to slope forwards, pitching me into an ever-faster sprint that now included not only tree trunks, low lying branches and every kind of bush and shrub, but boulders, rocky outcroppings and great, big, massive stair cases.

In an instant I became aware of just how many bony joints my body was made of as I somersaulted and tumbled along a steep procession of concrete edges.

In the films, after taking a tumble down a flight of stairs, the hero just gets up and carries on running, fighting and being the hero, as if there is a special way to roll down a staircase. But even with my Nooseman resilience I had never been more aware of things like shins, ankles, vertebrae, elbow joints and pelvis.

At the top of the stairs looking down at me was Cheshire.

"That was very impressive," she said.

"Am I still being chased?" I groaned.

"No," she said, "Turns out you're neither brave nor cowardly."

Things inside me crunched back into place as I climbed to my feet and dusted myself off.

"What am I then?"

"A bloody moron," she said, "But as luck would have it this is the next stop."

"Why is it that all women in my life seem to end up talking to me the same way?" I asked, pressing a hand to the side of my neck and encouraging a vertebra to go home.

"Because we all think you're a dick." She answered gliding passed me, "Or it's just bad writing."

The stairs led down to an iron door with the words WELCOME across them in raised letters. Rust may have streaked the corners but it opened on oiled hinges when Cheshire used a key on it. It swung inwards and banged against the inside wall and that booming sound echoed around a darkened interior.

She would never admit it, but I saw Cheshire swallow hard as she entered the dark.

Anxiously trying not to show my fear, I followed.

The door closed behind us and the lights came on revealing we were in a concrete corridor lightened by caged light bulbs across the upper edges. It was dry in here and the light was warm - it filled me with a sense of relief.

"Ah," I said, "It makes sense. The brave are chased by monsters to here and the cowards, having seen their friends pursued, are gathered up and brought here as well. They are reunited in a warm, dry place with lots of light where they are reassured."

Cheshire, unable to float due to the low ceiling gave me a sideways look, "You understand this all quite well."

I didn't comment but was looking down the lengthy corridor at a simple wooden door at the far end. Nothing fancy about it, a generic door, painted light-blue with an office-style handle that looked exactly like the kind of doors seen in nurseries and schools. It would seem that irrespective of which world you were in these doors were used in the same kind of places.

"I'm going to hate what's behind that door, aren't I?" I asked as we walked towards it.

Cheshire, walking ahead of me said, "Yes. But can you imagine the hope that the children are feeling now? It doesn't take a lot to rattle a young mind, an unexpected fright and a break of routine is enough to shatter their little lives. They'd see this door and think of all those times there was an adult who wanted to look after them, make them safe and quiet. All those toys they could sit down and play with."

We got to the door but before Cheshire opened it, she said, "Donnie, it's important that you know that the Queen of Hats wanted you to see this, it is her wish. Before we go in can you remember that for me?"

"I'll try to keep it in mind," I said.

"It's just that I don't know what is actually behind this door," she admitted.

"How interesting," I said, but chose not to mention that I had already noticed that the faded, muddied shoe prints on the floor all led in one direction and not the other.

Cheshire was staring at the door, her hands clasped together in front of her chest. She didn't look like she wanted to open the door, so I did.

Sometimes you cannot let yourself turn away.

Sometimes you have to face the horrors one person can do to another. Long after Cheshire had fled from that room, her weeping echoing down the corridor to my back, I stood there. With my hand on the door I memorized every detail: those terribly recognizable shapes, the stories that those splatters and puddles told, the heavy smells that revealed more than I wanted to know. The room had been decorated like a school classroom, the walls covered in hand drawings in crayons of homes, houses, colourful crayon families with colourful crayon hair.

The Hare would bring them in and would have them draw pictures of their homes and their families. Then he would tie them to their chairs and desks.

Select them one by one and take them into the back room.
The backroom, the small room just behind the teacher's desk, just around the corner. Years of living in Purgatory had given me ways of seeing things. He would lead them in there. Make them scream. Bring them out, sit them down again and let the other girls and boys in the class see what had happened.
Then he would select the next one.

My stomach emptied itself suddenly, the vomit punching the roof of my mouth and coming out my nose.
Ten minutes later I joined Cheshire at the entrance, she was sat on the steps her face in her hands, her tail curled around her waist.

"I swear to you Donnie, I didn't know," she whimpered, "I swear I didn't know it was that bad."

"What did you believe he was doing with them after he took them into that room?" I asked her. I was surprised with my own tone of voice. Surprised it was so calm, so steady.

"I never asked myself that," she admitted, "But I'm glad for what you did. I'm glad. Are you glad?"

"Come along," I said, walking up the stairs, "I guess it is time you took me to see this Queen of Hats."

"Yes." Cheshire said.

8.

"Is he a guest or a prisoner?" a squeaky voice asked somewhere ahead of me in the murky darkness. Another voice, very similarly annoying responded, "Does it matter?"

"Well," the first voice said haughtily, "If he's a guest or a prisoner it'd affect us wouldn't it?"

"How so?"

"We'd either be a guard or a valet."

"He is chained and sitting in a prison cell!"

"Yes, but there are some places where you can pay for this kind of service!"

"Do you think he's paying?"

"I don't know, shall I ask?"

"I don't know. Do you want to ask?"

"No... not really."

"Why not?"

"I'm not sure. I don't know if he's a prisoner or a guest."

I had been awake for a while and had no recollection of falling asleep in the first place. But I couldn't let them carry on like this. They were getting highly agitated with each other, so to show the pair of them that I was awake I gave an overly loud gasp and cried, "The Tweedle brothers!"

"By the skies, he knows who we are, Dum!"

"Of course, he does Dee, he *was* here before!"

"Was he a guest or a prisoner then?"

"I don't know...I think he was in chains for a little bit, but that wasn't in a cell was it?"

"No," I said, opening my eyes and looking around, "It was handcuffs and in the Red Queen's bedroom. This does look familiar though."
I was in a metal cage, a cube with four walls and a ceiling that had jagged spikes and blades facing inwards. The excessive chains wrapped around my wrists, upper arms, legs and ankles were all bolted to the floor of the cage. That someone thought I warranted such a high number of heavy chains was quite flattering. On the outside of the cage looking in were two very round characters wearing school uniforms, school caps and very, very dull expressions.

"Excuse me sir," one of them asked, "Are you a guest or a prisoner this time?"
I chuckled. The Tweedle brothers had been a good laugh when I was here last. Again, from what memories I had of the last time I was here, the Tweedle Brothers had been fabulous drinking buddies. Able to abide an unusual amount of alcohol while retaining the same level of ideocratic stupidity before summarily passing out and rolling down a hill.

"Well," I said in answer, "I'm naked and tied up so it could be either. Why don't you ask someone?"

"Oh, you mean a secondary outsourced opinion?" TweedleDum asked

"A neutral second opinion?" TweedleDee added.

"There we go boys," I said, "There is your solution. Go get me that secondary opinion."
In a rolling sort of movement, the brothers dropped their guarding weapons which consisted of a broom

stick and a spatula each and rushed out of the dungeons.

In the silence that followed, I peered around. The dungeons had a lot of empty alcoves, hollowed out without any bars. The only actual cell was the one I was in. Clearly, they did not massively condone the keeping of prisoners.

"I know you're there," I said, my voice echoing around the dark space, "You can come out."

A moment passed, then there was a small throat clearing, a shuffle in the darkness and someone stepped out of the shadows.

"How did you know I was here?" Alice asked.

"Jeez," I said, sagging, "I didn't, I was taking a chance. *You're* the traitor?"

Her thin, perfect eyebrows lifted in surprise, she drew back her red hood and stepped up to the cage, "Traitor?"

"Well, you are definitely not a prisoner," I said.

"It's not what you think," she told me.

"I know it's not what I think! I thought it was Cheshire who was bringing me to the Queen. But it's you? How does that work anyway, you are working with Cheshire?"

Alice's face went blank, as if any feeling of regret just washed off her. Her jaw set firmly in an expression I often see people use. Usually, after I've let my mouth off the leash, and it's gone running off along the beach.

"I'm fulfilling my contract." She said, "I need to get The Rabbit, and an exchange is the only way to do it."

"You're exchanging Kaben?" I asked, gob smacked.

Alice blinked, "No, you idiot. I'm exchanging you. Kaben is locked up downstairs."

I shook my head disapprovingly, "You'd lock up your own dog."

"It was with in his best interest," she said, "He will forgive me. I'm his mistress after all."

I spat on the floor, "I don't believe you. He could be dead for all I know. He could be just another toy in your game."

To prove her point she strode, and I hated myself for how I watched her buttocks move beneath that cloak, to a large iron door in one of the walls and unlocked it. She pulled the heavy door open with some effort. I could hear the desperate whining below.

"Kaben?" I called.

"Donnie!?" he cried, "Donnie, I can't handle this! They've got me in a tiny hole and it's killing me, I'm choking in here can you get me out!?"

"I'm afraid not, I'm prisoner too."

"Filthy scum! Do you know what they've done to my Mistress?"

I looked at Alice and she held my gaze for a moment before calling down, "I'm here, Kaben. I am fulfilling the contract and will be down to collect you soon. Can you be patient?"

"Mistress? Mistress!? Thank heavens you're safe. Do you need me to help you?"

"No no," she said, "You stay down there. Do not hurt yourself."

"Kaben!" I called, "I want you to escape and come save me, you owe me remember? I saved Alice from the Hare!"

The wolf man roared, "You did! You saved my Mistress! I will! I will escape and come save you, Donnie! I will do it for her!"

Alice pushed the door shut and thrust the latch down furiously, "You bastard," she said, pointing at the door, "He could kill himself now trying to escape! How could you be so selfish?"

"You haven't been paying much attention, have you?" I asked in earnest.

She walked up to the cage and put her hands on the bars. She took a breath and abruptly changed the subject, "You know I loved you for a time?"

"Yeah I loved you to," I said, "But that moment passed, and I guess you cleaned up the mess."

"It was more than just a moment, but it's done now. It's funny how easily love can turn to hate. Almost as if they are the same thing, just from a different perspective."

I tried to shift position but couldn't, the chains were bound so tight that I couldn't move at all. I sighed, "What now Alice? What happens now?"

"The Queen of Hats wants to meet you."

She walked to the dungeon door and banged on it with a fist. It swung open and a dozen guards entered the dungeon. Tall things they were. Long robotic legs whirled and hummed on every step, steam hissing out of their joints as they trundled forward. At the ends of their long arms were weapons, on one side the barrel of an oversized gun and the other a large sword. I saw that they could interchange these with animatronic hands that were currently not in use, instead they were fastened backwards, clinging onto the metal forearms. They were robots, save for what served as their heads.

"That is disgusting."

Where their heads should have been were glass jars with heads floating in them. These distorted visages, with the diamond tattoo of the red queen on their cheeks, floated in pickled vinegar coloured liquid. They were conscious and aware, an assortment of wires and tubes led from their heads down into the mechanics below. What was truly disturbing was that none of them possessed a jaw bone. As if they had been removed to stop them from speaking or perhaps their executioner had very poor aim with his axe.

"I will agree with you on that," Alice said, "Do you recognize these men?"

"How could I?" I asked.

One of them detached from the regiment and unlocked the cage door, he swung it open and extended an arm at me. Some kind of energy field emanated from that limb because it made my fillings ache and the chains around me unfastened themselves and slunk meekly to the floor. I couldn't stand upright because of the downward facing blades above, designed to keep occupants in a kneeling position so I waited obstinately until Alice said.

"You will have to crawl out."

"I'd rather be dragged out," I replied, "I have my prid- hmph!"

The guard had the good form to deposit me onto my feet instead of just dropping me onto my head and I brushed myself down and said, "Thank you."

"These guards are fairly pragmatic," Alice explained.

"Good habit to have when you can't talk," I said, "Now can I have some clothes before I see the Queen? I have my dignity you know."

"You may as well let that go right away," Alice said, "You won't keep it long."

The castle was warm, the floor a little colder than the air around it, but it wasn't entirely unpleasant walking down the corridors guarded on all sides by big warm machines that spat out hot steam. Alice kept glancing my way as we walked.

"You looked perplexed Alice," I said helpfully, "What's up?"

"You don't seem angry," she commented, "Do you not fear death?"

"In my career I've been hung, strangled, shot in the head- which I will say, having your brains splattered around a room is quite enlightening- burned and even harpooned." I pointed out quite a crater shaped hole the size of a plate that was on both sides of my torso, "Yes. That harpoon hurt."

"You have grown your collection of sizeable scars. Have you considered collecting stamps instead?"

"My point is that I don't fear death, what I fear is living with what I've seen."

For a second, she looked genuinely moved and then laughed out loud, "That line would have been pretty good if you hadn't been the one to say it! No come on seriously, why aren't you angry?"

I shrugged, "The night is young. Let's see what happens."

After passing through a number of chambers with staircases leading off in different directions and a morbid chamber where the walls were all covered in paintings of beheaded "champions", we entered a vast hall with pillars of stone supporting a high arching ceiling. Curtains hung by the tall windows depicting red and white diamonds, the carpets on the floor were red and white too and the servants that stood along the central carpet leading up to the stairs, which in turn led up to the double thrones, were also dressed in red and white.

And seated on the throne, was the Queen of Hats... also in red and white.

"At least that explains the colour design," I said, as one of the guards poked me in the back. I walked forward, feeling exposed for the first time during the day because there were more guards standing at the perimeter of the hall, each armed with wickedly-shaped blades that suggested they were skilled at taking heads and currently, I had two on show.

Alice walked ahead and said in a loud voice that carried across the hall, "Your Majesty, as promised I have brought you a replacement."

The Queen of Hats sat upon a tall-backed throne of white gold and red upholstery dressed in a royal gown that was interchanging red and white horizontal stripes, making her look ever so slightly like a candy stick. The gown was tied with a brooch across the chest and had a high collar that almost reached the brim of her very large top hat. Almost mechanical in nature, in the same steampunk fashion as the guards, the hat itself was moving. Small and intricate pieces of machinery ran around the entirety of the hat and moved it with a mechanical life of its own.

The woman beneath the hat was not to be disregarded though, for I recognized her. Her hair was the brilliant blonde that had once been associated so firmly with the Alice of legend and framed her face in curls and twirls. Her face was painted one half red and the other half white and her body, from tip of toe to throat was tattooed with red rune shapes.

"Eve." I said.

"You will address the Queen of Hats as your Majesty, you wretched creature!"

The Rabbit walked into view and took up a station at the foot of the throne stairs. A tall man, brilliantly dressed in an exquisite grey three-piece suit, with wonderfully polished brown leather shoes. He stood with a regally straight back and as he spoke from one hand hung a pocket watch. The other, the one he currently pointed at me with, had a very handsome signet ring on the ring finger. His face was hidden behind a porcelain rabbit's face mask, which covered it from the nose up, leaving his bottom jaw exposed, a feature that was dominated by an impressively dimpled chin. He could have been called masculine, but as if to chip away at this, one of the ears was bent half way to give the mask a severe cuteness which made him look as homosexual as intimidating.

"Hehe, look at this guy, I bet he shaves his ball sack," I giggled.

"You will not speak until given permission by her Majesty the Queen of Hats!"

I was inclined to obey that time as there were just too many sharp objects around for me to argue.

The Queen spoke then, her voice amplified by the mechanisms of the Hat, "Alice, my dear, please come forward."

Without looking my way, Alice approached, her hands held out to her side to show she was unarmed. The Rabbit nevertheless positioned himself at the foot of the stairs, putting himself directly in her way should she try to bolt up them. Seeing her near him though, put his size into perspective, he must have been close on seven feet tall!

"Step aside Mr. Rabbit," the Queen commanded, "Alice will not try and hurt me. She has a bounty to collect after all."

The Rabbit reluctantly turned to the side which allowed Alice to speak to the Queen without him sacrificing his position as guard between them.

"Alice, please inform me why you believe that this person would be suitable to replace The Rabbit?"

Alice bowed her head, "This is the former Ambassador of Norwich, the Fine City of Purgatory. He is the one chosen to delegate between humans, the Late, the Lost and the Otherwise."

"Politics of the outside world mean very little to us here," The Queen said, not in an unkindly way but a direct way, "Try again."

"He is a Nooseman," Alice added smoothly.

"Do you possess his rope?" The Queen asked.

"No," Alice said, her voice faltering slightly.

"Then how useful can a Nooseman be to me? Without his noose I cannot control him, and he will be at the will of someone else. Try again silly girl and this time make it good."

"He has been here before," Alice said, "He was the cause of the Great Sorrow that this land suffered, before your Majesty took the throne."

The Queen frowned and her eyes left Alice and looked over at me, she leant an elbow on the arm of her throne and said, "Is this true, Cheshire?"

The cat appeared at her side, floating cross-legged in mid-air, her coat and her tail hanging a foot off the floor. Her face did not convey the things we had seen behind the March Hare's door.

"Yes, your Grace it is true."

The Queen brought her fingertips to her lips and passed her gaze over my entire body, "He carries many scars," she said, "The Rabbit has none."

"Your Majesty," Alice said, "His scars run deep, but each tells a story. He is a man of substance."

I giggled and choked on my own spit at what Alice had said and turned away to hide my coughing.

"Very well," The Queen said, "That is one good point. But you will need another for me to release The Rabbit."

"Pardon me, your Queenship," I said, raising a hand, "May I speak?"

The entire assembly in the hall turned as one to face me, the sudden impact of all their gazes felt like being buffeted by a physical wave.

"Did you not hear me before? Horrible little man!" The Rabbit roared in anger, "You will address the Queen of Hats as your Majesty or Your Grace or I will personally cut off..."

"Oh! Do shut up!" the Queen snapped, she raised a hand and beckoned me forward with a finger, "You may approach, potential slave of mine."

I padded forward, seeing that Cheshire had about her eyes a fearful look of what I was going to say, also Alice stood quite rigidly. The closer I got to The Rabbit the bigger he became, not only was he easily seven feet tall without the bunny ears, but he was also exceptionally wide at the shoulders.

"Hi, your Majesty," I said, "Does my opinion count at all in this matter?"

"Well that depends," the Queen said loftily, "On what your opinion is."

"Well, I was tricked into coming here," I explained, "Told that I would be a sort of a guide as I've been here before. But it was all a ruse, I had no idea that Alice's plan was to replace this..." I glanced up to The Rabbit with what I hoped was a suitably intimidated look, "Mountain of a man with me. I fear that I would probably be inadequate in any regard."

"Don't sell yourself short," The Queen said, "While The Rabbit is certainly hung like an elephant's leg, he is very short on conversation and I have heard every one of his stories multiple times. I grow bored of fantastic sex and would be happy to trade it for something average if it came with good conversation and pillow talk."

I couldn't help myself, "I would not call my sex average, your Majesty," I said, "Ask these two what I am like in bed."

The Queen looked at Alice and then at Cheshire with interest, "Oh really? You both have been there?"

Cheshire, the only one who could get out of here fast enough should things go south took the chance and answered, "Yes, your Grace."

The Queen adjusted her position on the throne, "Oh, how very interesting. I *love* a good gossip, so tell me, how was he?"

"He is amazing in bed," Cheshire answered, giving me a wink, "Although I do confess while he was here not once did, we ever actually do it in the bedroom."

The Queen clapped her hands together in delight, "Oh, how wonderful! An adventurous lover then? And you Alice?"

"I only had the pleasure of sampling him over one night your Majesty," Alice said, "But I can assure you not only did I get no sleep at all, but I could scarcely walk the next morning."

The Queen bit her bottom lip and beamed at me. I rubbed my eyes and said, "I wish I hadn't said anything your Majesty. Look, I am sorry but my point remains that I don't want to stay. I was tricked into coming here, does that not count for something?"

"Of course it does," The Queen said, "Whoever tricked you will have their heads twisted and lobbed from their bodies. Was it Alice? Cheshire?"

"Well, it wasn't Alice who tricked me first so I don't think she should lose her head," I said, "I don't think anyone should lose their head over this. I actually just want to leave in peace."

"Who tricked you if it wasn't them?" The Queen asked.

"I am afraid I am not at liberty to tell you," I said, adding lamely at the end, "Your Majesty."

"Your Queen has asked you a direct question," The Rabbit said, stepping forward with a grotesque speed and picking me up into the air by the throat. He shook me casually as he spoke, "You will answer her directly or I will squeeze your neck so hard your head pops."

"Could get awfully messy," I managed to say, "But no."

"Madam Thankeron," Alice said loudly, "He was tricked by Madam Thankeron."

The Rabbit dropped me at the mention of the name and I landed hard on my rear, I rubbed my neck and said, "Alice, you're an idiot."

The Queen and The Rabbit exchanged looks. She stood up and this alone caused a rippling movement throughout the hall as everyone took a knee, out of rebellious impulse I stood up instead. She strode down the stairs, walking passed Alice and The Rabbit and in a smooth movement backhanded me.

I can honestly say, up until that point at least, I've never been hit so hard.

It wasn't the physical force behind it. Like a mother who grabs the collar of her child and delivers a spanking that is never forgotten into adulthood. The back of her hand was felt not just by me, but by all of me; it was felt all the way back through my ancestors with a sting that would last all the way up my descendants. The sting of it rang through time.

Suddenly, I was a child again, a five-year-old boy who had discovered the boundary of a parent's patience and that this boundary line is patrolled by five fingers and a palm. I felt panic-stricken and shocked; guilty of breaking something cherished, of forcing a mother to discipline her own child. The tears that came streaked lines in the dirt of the dungeon to reveal a vapid blush on my cheeks, and I bit my bottom lip to stop it from trembling.

"You see," she said quietly and just to me, "You are but a man to me and I am your Mother, the Mother of All Men, the first in the long line. You are connected to me as surely as you are connected to that noose that binds your spirit and your body, but if I wanted to I could break you down to dust."

I stared at the floor, the only place free of the condemning and pitying gazes of the people around me. The beast inside me had changed, the monster that I kept at bay at all times that wanted to rip free and destroy the world had suddenly shifted its composition and was now a pathetic thing trembling in the corner of my mind. I longed for my mother's touch, I feared abandonment and she was right, in that instant I would have done anything she had asked if she would just reach out and embrace me to her bosom.

"Your opinion means nothing to me you see," she added, "You are mine after all, aren't you?"

I bit my lip hard to stop me from blubbering and murmured an affirmative sound.

"Do you love me?" she asked.

I nodded, tears dripping from my chin now and pattering onto the carpet. She spoke softly again; her breath cool against the burning pain of my cheek. I wanted to fling my arms around her and beg her forgiveness, beg her to not send me away. I wanted to call her Mommy.

"Now, what am I going to do with you?" she asked, whispering intimately in my ear, "How shall you make this up to me? This grievous sin of yours..."

"Sin?" I asked.

"Yes... you fucked the Mother of Monsters, didn't you?"

Lilith. Did she have the same power of control over the monsters that existed in the world? Those creatures of the Otherwise, those beasts and demons that lurked and thrived in my city. Did Lilith control them like Eve controlled me?

"I did," I answered, feeling a cool calmness wash over me from the nape of my neck down. Whatever I possessed as a mind, rose above the stormy clouds of my Oedipus emotions and went into orbit above them. Then, like an astronaut having his perspective changed by that first sight of the curvature of the Earth, I felt a deep, satisfying enlightenment. I turned my face to The Queen of Hats, Eve, the Mother of all Men and said:

"I fucked the Mother of Monsters and then I didn't call her back. What makes you think you are different?"

Too old to be taken by surprise easily, her eyes narrowed with interest at the sudden change of script.

She said, "I would have you eating out of the palm of my hand, you'd be like a puppy to me."

I took a deep and completely uninterrupted breath and looked around the vast hall with a clear perspective. I saw Cheshire peeking out from behind the throne, I saw Alice, her eyes wide with uncertainty, The Rabbit standing with his rigidly straight back, the pocket watch clasped tightly in his fist. Then back to the Queen of Hats, her ethereal blue eyes glared out from the face paint, her tattoos shimmered red with anger, her locks of hair seemed to radiate power, but it had lost its magic. I had seen the wires behind the light show, I had seen the hamster in the wheel, I was no longer spellbound.

"Dear Mother," I said with a sigh, "You have no control over me and I respectfully decline your offer. I'm going home."

9.

And, I woke up in the dungeon again.

I lifted my head and groaned at the bruise across the side of my face. Cheshire was sitting above the floor on the other side of the bars, her legs crossed, her elbows on her knees her chin in her hands. Her tail snaked beneath her within the cone-like tarp of her coat.

"I really need to stop being knocked out," I said, "It's bound to cause a brain tumor or something."

"It makes for a very convenient narrative break," Cheshire said, "Moves the story along nicely."

I cast her a suspicious eye, "Wow, that's usually something I would say."

She shrugged her shoulders, if this is ever made into a film, she would probably look at the camera and wink or blow a kiss to the audience.

"At least you're not chained up," Cheshire said.

"It's something at least," I agreed, rolling onto my back and looking up at the vicious spikes pointing down at me, "Not much though. What do you want Cheshire?"

"I've come to ask you a favour," she said.

"Do you think I'm in a position to grant any favours?" I asked, "Besides, I can't help feeling that you conned me along with everyone else."

"I never had an allegiance with you," she said, "I told you I was sent to bring you to the Queen of Hats; Alice had to replace The Rabbit, it's not my fault that you didn't put two and two together."

"I'm an idiot, haven't you realized?" I asked.

"You're smarter than you pretend," she said.

"People often make that mistake," I commented, reaching up and flicking my finger against one of the spikes, it gave a satisfactory *ding* and then without warning dislodged and slammed into the floor where I had been lying. From the side of the cage I cried out, "Whaaaaaaaa!"

The blade stayed there for a moment before slowly, as if it wanted to make sure I had taken notice, it was pulled back into the ceiling.

"See!?" I said to Cheshire.

The cat didn't argue with the evidence but persisted, "Still, I need to ask you this favour. Will you at least hear me out?"

"Sure," I said, trying to find a place around the floor of the cage not directly under one of those spikes, "I don't have a choice."

"Ever since The Queen of Hats took power Wonderland has been a dark place, inharmonious and you cannot ignore that it is your fault that they were able to take power in the first place."

"They?" I commented, "The Rabbit is the Queen's bitch,"

"Aren't all men to their queens?" Cheshire asked innocently.

I was about to argue but didn't see the point. She continued:

"It's your fault, and so you have to be the one to fix things. It's only fair after all- it's not much of a favour to ask and if you're honest with yourself, you probably came back in the hope that you could fix things."

"I can't do anything while in prison," I said.

"Accept the Queen's offer," Cheshire said.

"She doesn't really want me,"

"Oh, come on Donnie," Cheshire said, lying herself flat upon the invisible floor she lay on, propping her chin up on her elbows, "You know how to seduce a woman... convince The Queen that you want to stay here with her. Let Alice complete her contract and once sorted, plan your escape. You escaped Wonderland once before and you can do it again."

"I don't have my knob," I said.

Her eyes drifted down away from my face.

"My door knob, Cheshire, my door knob! I need it to escape Wonderland."

Her eyes lingered and she smiled, dug around in her coat pocket and produced a copper ball, "You mean this knob?"

"Well, you sneaky little pussy cat!"

She tipped her top hat to me, "So, you will do this for me?"

I thought about it for a moment, "Okay, but I need a favour from you. Kaben needs to be freed."

"Didn't expect you to be taken with the wolf man," she said.

"Whatever. Once he is out of Wonderland, I will do this favour for you,"

"Seems fair, can anyone use this knob?"

"No," I said, frowning, "The knob was made especially for me."

She put the sphere back into her pocket and said, "In that case, here is the deal: I will liberate your dog man friend and take him somewhere else in

Wonderland. I will give you back your knob and you will agree to the terms of The Queen of Hats to replace The Rabbit- after which you can escape."
It seemed like a clear opportunity.

Well, I thought, as I lowered myself gingerly into the hot bath, this isn't at all that bad.

Firstly, the bathtub was the size of a boat, three of me could have floated on our backs in the water. Made of solid porcelain lined with gold at the top, it stood upon golden lion paws on a podium of marble in a bathroom with more floor space than my own apartment (which is spacious, and stylishly decorated).

The ceiling arched to a central oculus showing the soupy sky above and around the keystones of the arch were flamed torches providing the light of a thousand candles. There were towels, robes and slippers of thick cotton on a golden trestle table at the corner and while the room itself dripped of verbose extravagance; it was the set of faucets that topped the cake for me. Two golden carps stood sentinel six feet away and at a twist of a tap atop the bathtub rim they spewed streams of liquid from their mouths that arched the distance between us and landed in the bath with a gurgle.

I had played with it during the first bath I had, which had left the bathtub with a thick rim of black sludge of dirt from the dungeon. I had then allowed the bathroom servants to come in and clean it and run another bath.
Getting myself comfortable I extended both arms on either side so that my fingertips touched the brim of

the bath and allowed myself to float on the surface. Like this I drifted, not really thinking of anything, let alone thinking of how I was going to escape. In comparison, I'm sure you would have been deep in a plot to escape, wouldn't you? But no, I was just enjoying the bath.

I heard the handles to the bathroom doors twist and the thick wooden panels swing open. Felt the soft movement of air across my wet torso as the cold air outside met the steaming sauna air inside. The doors closed without any words being spoken and thanks to the amplifying nature of water, I distinctly heard the light footsteps of the pair of people who had entered.

My mental targeting system located and zoned in on the different weapons I could find in the bathroom, the towels, the chairs in the side line, the soap basket that could be snapped off the bathtub side. Meanwhile, I tracked the footsteps as one person went to the head of the bathtub and the other went to the side.

Years of training at one of the leading schools of Assassins when I was an impressionable youngster had equipped me with skills that will always be at my disposal. Tactics and strategies, plans and mechanisms blasted through my brain while my mind stayed as cool and as calm as a gentle pond, ready to accept whatever came.

Fingertips against the rim of the bath and I heard their breathing for the first time.

Female assassins. Of course. As a man I would have sensed male assassins as soon as they entered into the bathroom, but females would always be welcome and so I wouldn't notice them until it was theoretically too late. Whoever had sent them, knew me well.

"Are you awake?" one of them asked.

"Yes," I said, "Whatever you're planning on doing I would suggest you do it now, you may not get another chance."

They took the warning to heart with an enthusiastic, "Okay."

As naked as the day they were born the two women climbed into the tub with me, a simple enough gesture that left me spluttering as they sank in giggling with each other.

One had strawberry red hair and silver eyes with the kind of milky white flesh that is so unblemished it glows and the other was a dusky brown, with chocolate brown eyes and hair as white as snow, tied up in a high pony tail.

"Hello ladies," I said, adjusting myself, "What the hell is going on?"

"We were sent to make sure you're comfortable," the red head said, "My name is Leandra and hers is Naomi."

Leandra and Naomi snuggled in closely and went straight to work, getting their hands between my legs. There was no fumbling here, they were very well trained with what they were doing. However, I gently pushed their hands away and said, "I'm sorry ladies, but I am only interested in The Queen of Hats, she is my chosen woman and you pair simply do not match her."

I climbed out of the bath and took up one of the towels and wiped myself down before slipping into one of the robes. The pair of them leaned their chins on their hands on the rim of the bathtub, looking like seductive sirens and lingered.

"I am not joking," I said, tying the robe belt around my midriff, "Cheshire."

Exactly the same expression appeared on both of their faces, then in an explosion of purple smoke Cheshire appeared in their stead, lying naked in the bathtub her tail swinging wetly above her perfect bubble buttocks and long legs. She tipped her top hat back on her head and pouted, "How did you know?"

"Please," I said, walking to the drinks cabinet. Yes, there was a drink cabinet in the bathroom and you actually had to walk over to it. "I never forget a woman once I've been with her. So, you can report back to the Queen that I am faithfully hers."

I went and sat down in one of the leather sofas at the far end of the bathroom and sipped the Wonderland version of rum. It wasn't bad. In the bathtub Cheshire dove under the water and poofed into existence draped out across me on the sofa.

"And put some clothes on," I said, unable not to spy the essentials. Save for her paws and tail, Cheshire was entirely hairless save for a single strip of purple hair leading down to her tiny packaged slit. She poofed and reappeared at the drink's cabinet clothed.

"Try the rum, it's a little too sweet but not too bad," I said.

"I know what the rum tastes like in Wonderland," she said, "You'll be happy to know that I freed Kaben, as agreed. But he was ardent that he was going to come and rescue you."

"That's convenient, considering that he can't get out of Wonderland without me. What about The Rabbit and Alice?"

Cheshire strode back to the sofa and perched on its arm, "There is a ceremony that needs to happen for you to become The Rabbit. Alice needs to be there too, once it is done, she will take The Rabbit and leave Wonderland and you will be at the beck and call of the Queen of Hats."

"How will they leave Wonderland?"

"The Queen of Hats has permitted it," she said, sipping her drink.

I leaned back and stared up at the torch light above me, "Could Kaben go back with Alice?"

"Yes," Cheshire said.

"To seal the deal between us, can you make sure that he is with her?"

The cat nodded, "Aye, that is certainly possible. But I will only do that once you're The Rabbit, before that and I'm doing too much for free."

"But, otherwise, I have your word?"

She winked at me, "Yes."

The ceremony was not held in the grand hall but rather in an underground chamber where the lighting was all hospital-morgue green, the walls tiled and the floor hash tagged with steel drainage grates. A room noticeably wider than tall, The Rabbit, standing beside the Queen's throne would have crushed his ears against it if he had but gone on his tiptoes. The lights were positioned so that all those present and standing around the edges cast long shadows towards the center.

"I should warn you there has been a development from this afternoon's little chat," Cheshire said, as we first entered.

"What's happened?"

"Kaben is not in Wonderland," she said, "I have no idea where he is."

"Could he be dead?" I asked.

"Bit of a harsh assumption isn't it?" she said.

"Have you seen what you call a fucking Caterpillar?" I retorted.

"I don't think so but he could be anywhere," she said. But our conversation couldn't continue because we had properly entered the chamber and people were looking at me.

My suit had been washed and prepared for me and the new linen shirt they gave me was particularly fetching and smelt fresh like starch and vanilla. It felt good to be back in a clean suit. I had been amazed at how filthy it had managed to get during our short trip through the forest. In forty pages or less it had been totally ham shanked.

I did my best to look as casually confident as possible but the fact that there was a bathtub in the middle of the room within the center of a square section of grates disturbed me greatly. This wasn't a similar bathtub to what I had enjoyed previously; this was a bathtub that looked as if it had been picked up from a back garden after being left leaning against the fence. It was stained yellow and was filled with some kind of clear liquid.

If there is a chair in the middle of a room where you are expected, you can expect to sit in it. But did they expect me to get into the bathtub?

The Queen of Hats seemed to gain interest in the proceedings as I entered and without anyone to escort me, I was left to my own devices, as I suppose was Cheshire's plan.

"Your Majesty," I said, offering a short bow to her and then adding, "Hello, Rabbit."

"I have been looking forward to this," The Queen said.

I gave her my best smile and counted the guards around me. There were seventeen in total in the chamber, those that were armed at least. There were some servants dotted around, almost unseen in the dim lighting. I asked, "I am afraid that I am unfamiliar with the ceremony, your Grace. I hope you will not judge me badly for it."

"Of course not," she said, "This is a fair court. Mr. Rabbit, perhaps you could direct your potential replacement in these affairs?"

The Rabbit bowed to his queen and walked up to where I stood, and, in a voice that I would almost describe as helpful, he said, "In the bathtub there is the Queen of Hat's elixir."

"Oh, is that what that is?" I asked.

"Indeed, and that on the rim of the bathtub is a cup."

It took a moment for me to realize what he wasn't saying. I pointed, "You want me to empty that bathtub with a cup?"

"Yes," he said.

"Into where? The grates?"

"No!" he replied, laughing jovially. It was a rich and full laugh and it got many of the assembled court chortling along. Even the queen joined in on the joyous mockery of such a silly question. He wiped his nose, "You are to empty it by drinking it."

"But... correct me if I'm wrong... but that's her Majesty's...?"

"Periurethral expellant," he said, helpfully.
I stepped away from him, my hand on my mouth, "That's her...?"

"Yes. It is important that The Rabbit acquire a taste for the Queen's elixir and this proves to be a very good time to start."

"Anything, else?" I asked.

"No, just that," he said with a grin, "On you go." He shoved me forward and I approached the bathtub cautiously. I was a man who appreciated a woman's ability to soak the bedsheets. But, as with many things, it all depends on the setting. The cup sitting on the rim of the bathtub looked distressingly small, whereas the nearer I got to the tub I saw it was distressingly full.

I could see my reflection in the thick watery substance. To my credit I had managed to keep a face that suggested I was alright with the whole situation.

"Your Majesty," I said, with a smile and another short bow, "I am humbled by your gift."
She returned my gesture with a smile and said, "Please enjoy. Once the tub is empty Mr. Rabbit will be released and allowed to leave with your friend Alice."

I looked around the assembled court, "Where is Alice, your Majesty? I was hoping to see her here for the ceremony?"

The Queen waved a hand as if it didn't concern her, "This is not a matter for Alice. This is between you and me, my dear man. I would like to suggest that you don't keep me waiting."

I gave a little bow, "I would like to take my time," I said, "I believe I will remember this moment for the rest of my life."

This seemed to satisfy her somewhat and with her eyes glowing from beneath the shadow of her hat, she paid close attention as I picked up the cup and dipped it into the liquid.

It was viscous and thicker than water and felt heavier in the cup as I brought it up. For the whole journey from tub to my lips I was waiting for someone to stop me, to tell me this was all just a distasteful prank and that I didn't actually have to drink this.

The rim of the cup touched my lips and the liquid on the outside of it made them itch.

Every gaze in this room was on me and this cup and I was tipping it to taste the first of what was to be many cupfuls of this liquid when I heard the long, high noted howl of Kaben. It reverberated off the walls, it echoed down the corridors and it got everyone's head turning in concern.

"He's come for me!" I shouted, hurling the cup to the ground and sending its liquid splashing through the grate.

The Rabbit swung for my head and I ducked under his blow and with the flat of my hand I delivered a sharp, merciless blow to his crotch that doubled him over.

I spun, pointing a finger at the Queen of Hats who was watching serenely, leaning on the arm of her throne, her index finger pressed against the side of her face beside her eye while her middle finger stroked her bottom lip. Her face was almost entirely in shadow now, thanks to the hat and her hair.

"That is Kaben, your Grace!" I shouted, "The Big Bad Wolf and the terror of the forest! He is the shadow that lurks at your back, the cool breath on the nape of your neck. He is terror and darkness and rage and he is here to take lives, to spill blood and leave his legend written upon the corpse of this castle when he is done!"

The howl shook the walls again and I paused, basking in the dramatic effect of it all.

"And do you know what makes him so terrifying?" I asked loudly, taking hold of the bathtub with both hands around the outer lip and heaving. At first it didn't move, then the liquid got the idea and tipping it over was just a matter of physics. "Is that you will never, ever know where he is!"

The howl was suddenly converted to a surprised splutter from directly below. The Queen started to laugh.

10.

Common belief is that torture is about pain, but it isn't, it is all about anticipation.
Depending on which side you're on, this can either be useful or, as it happens, torturous.
You also have to choose what kind of method you use. Select your mechanisms carefully and suitably for who you're going to be using them on. Hence why the German's used dentists while the Roman's used feathers - it's all down to how people anticipate what's going to happen to them.

I had lost count of the hours. I couldn't even judge it by the usually quite accurate bladder clock because I had already voided several times and was feeling as empty as an abandoned shoe. I was shackled to a plain wooden chair. The back of this chair was angled forward by several degrees so that my lower back was a cramping knot of muscle and I couldn't get any relief because my forehead was strapped to the top of it. And, because of the lights.
Facing me was a wall of light bulbs, each the size of an orange, blindingly bright they flashed every time I tried to adjust myself into a better position. They would flash up brightly then blink rapidly causing me to flinch.

That would have been sufficient but whoever had designed this was one exceptionally cruel artist.
Directly in front of me was a bulky box-like TV from the 90s, including old fashioned bunny ears on the top of it. The lights only came on when I tried to get some comfort, which meant they were off for shorter

periods of time now. But the TV was constantly on, playing the most torturous and horrific audio visual I could imagine.

A teenage boy with an absurd fish bowl haircut and the effeminate facial features of a Disney princess was singing, on a loop, the same three words, "Baby... baby... baby..."

Oh, the melody suggested that there was something else to come. The beat demanded it. But it was denied, and that part of my brain dedicated to the laws of four beats was left screaming in my head as every time it expected it to come it never came.

"Baby...baby.... baby..."

Oh, the high-pitched notes that this boy thing was able to hit sliced through my brain matter like knives, his cherubic facial features mocked me and swooned out of the TV screen threateningly. His dark eyebrows danced vindictively, and it had reached the point where I had vomited over my own bare knees as the tension turned to nausea and my body rebelled in the only way it could.

The folder binder that was crushing my lower back overcame my will and I sagged, and the lights blazed up, one long blast to get my eyelids shut and then a series of blinking fits that caused them to flutter maniacally. A migraine of epic proportions was narrated by this kid shrieking "Baby... baby... baby...."

Oh, it was the pause! That pause right after the last "Baby" that promised another word, another beat to it. It teased my anticipation for it but denied it.

I knew the song. It was the product of the pop-music-formula, which had been spewing out pop music for forty years. It fed a part of our brains addicted to a certain type of music. Designed as a template audio narcotic for the teenage generation it was meant to create generation gaps between parents and their children, hence facilitating a number of the new generation being misled and guided by the very servants of Satan.

People say that the Devil's greatest trick was convincing the world he didn't exist, it was actually popularizing music that was regurgitated shit to recruit entire legions of new followers. Of course, it only worked if you were a believer. Or something similar.

I had suspected this for a long time, but it was only when Satan accidentally let it slip over coffee that it was confirmed.

At the time I wasn't thinking any of this. No, all I could think about was those three words and that goddamned, aggravated missing fourth beat.

"Baby…. Baby… baby…"

Oh. Jeezus, I was crying. Snot oozing over my lips, mixing with the puke on my chin. My crying turned to desperate screaming, howling, barking and growling, I tried to get free, but those lights hit me like a physical blow that made me cry out. While "Baby…Baby…Baby" just taunted me.

The song had been well chosen. Carefully selected by Satan himself - it had been one of his triumphs and had stayed in the charts for so long that everyone in the world had been forced to hear it.

It was also by no means the only song they could have used. There were many different tunes that would have served the purpose, including ones

featuring wrecking balls, fat women on the stage singing hello, boring red heads singing about being homeless or home less than they want to be and bands determined to only go in one direction.
(In hindsight this paragraph won't make any sense to someone reading this in a hundred years when these series of diaries become prescribed reading for the school masses. You have my apologies, but I was being tortured.)

Every man has his breaking point. The will is only so strong and even mountains can be eroded by a patient stream.

My tongue didn't work. It was a slab of steak in my mouth that was too big for my cheeks. I tried to say something, but the words didn't come out the way they were meant to. I couldn't speak!

"I'm done!" I wanted to yell, I wanted to cry.

The lights blazed on and strobed again, causing me to flinch while:

"Baby…. baby….baby…."

Oh, I couldn't even surrender. So, I started to scream, convinced of the crazy notion I could scream myself to death.

You cannot die though, the voice in my head said.

You might have to speak up, I replied, it's awfully noisy in here at the moment.

I fell inwards at that point, imploded and found myself sitting on a brown leather Chesterfield staring at the brick wall in my apartment. Ah, my bare brick wall. My apartment walls are the typical plaster of egg-shell white and this is through all of the rooms save for this large perfectly-square patch, three metres wide and three metres tall that just popped up one day. On top of its strange appearance the brick work seemed to move when nobody was looking.

To my left, in a tall-backed Chesterfield, dressed in a white two-piece suit with a light grey waistcoat was the Devil. His elbows on the chair arms, his fingers steeped together in front of him.

"Hello Donnie," he said.

I twisted my head around the Chesterfield to see what was behind me. It was just my apartment. Same furniture, same dishes in the sink. It was a comforting if unoriginal sight. I looked down at myself and saw that I was suited again in my favourite black suit.

"I've never been dressed and naked so frequently," I said.

In the background that song clip still played, but it sounded very distant. Like a song being played from a car radio on the road outside and below us.

The devil looked away from the bare brick wall and scrutinized every corner of the room, "You must find it rewarding."

"I'm being tortured," I said, "How can this be rewarding?"

"Oh, we both know that you feel like you deserved it," the Devil said, putting his long, pianist fingers together again, "Anyway, I cannot stay long, unfortunately Wonderland is really beyond my limits. I am here on borrowed time."

"Borrowed from whom?" I asked.

"I called in some favours," he said.

"Or," I speculated, "Maybe you're just part of a hallucination?"

The Devil considered this, "This is possible, but wouldn't you have hallucinated someone or some other people... I can assure, however, that if you're expecting me to do anything weird or sexual that it will not end well for you."

I physically cringed from the idea, "Please tell me that that isn't going to happen."

"No. I am not a hallucination, but I am here to tell you that you have to find a way to get out of Wonderland... you cannot stay here."

The song clip was getting louder, as if the car and its radio were being lifted to the level of the window. At the same time car lights outside the Tudor style bay windows that wrapped around two of the walls of my living room started flashing outside. The car responsible was floating twenty feet above the road, its lights casting diamond-shaped grids across my walls.

"That is stating the obvious don't you think?" I asked.

"You were just trying to scream yourself to death," The Devil pointed out, "Do you not remember? I know your history and what you're capable of. You are more than willing to kill yourself to bugger up the plans of people who cross you. But you cannot die so easily, you can only scar. I think it's safe to say that you've pretty much destroyed your singing voice."

I had to admit; my throat was burning. Outside of my own head I suppose I was still doing my best to commit suicide via howling.

"You saying you have a plan for me?" I asked.

"We all have our plans for you," he said, "But I was the only one able to pop in and give you this nudge."

"And why were you able to do this?" I asked.

"Well, you've met God," the Devil said, shifting in his chair irritably, "You've seen how He isn't exactly – invested at the moment."

"Why you?" I pressed.

He smiled, "You have a beast inside you… a monster."

I didn't confirm or deny it, I really didn't need to. The beast inside uncoiled and I could feel it scratching at the mental cage. At the same time the music was getting louder and the flashes of lights were making me blink again.

"You can't have a Mother of Monsters without a Father."

"You're my Father?" I asked, my voice raising an octave, not out of fright but out of mirth.

"No," The Devil said, looking pointedly at the brick wall, "I am not your Father."

The dream broke and I woke up with a start, still shackled to that chair. The lights blazed, cutting into my eyeballs with renewed intensity and the unfinished song clip struck my ears like broken glass. My throat was ablaze, a tube of raw meat holding a pair of wrestling porcupines and my back had a pain that made me think of gears grinding in a truck. I wanted this to finish.

"Okay," I rasped, "I'm done."

With a boom the lights shut down and the darkness washed over me in a wave, the television stayed on for one last loop of the clip, "Baby… baby… baby… oh!"

Devious bastards, I thought as a mixture of relief and intense gratitude soothed my aching brain.
Some guards came in, unshackled me and helped me off of the chair and carried me out of the dark room. Fairly blind thanks to the flashing purple spots in front of my eyes, I was carried through a room that appeared grey and stood up in a shower. Someone told me to put my hands against the wall and a surge of water fell over me from above. I was scrubbed roughly with brushes smelling strongly of lavender.
Finally, I was led to a chamber that smelt of freshly-washed linen and sat down upon a bed with springs that groaned under my weight.

"Your clothes are next to you," the guard said, "Dress. The Rabbit will be down to visit you shortly."
I sat for a while, willing my eyes to adjust to the lack of strobe lights. Colours seemed to flash and bubble in and out of existence around the edges of everything I saw and in the centre of my vision, super imposed on everything was a square block of anti-colour and shape that was bellowing out that one damned lyric.

I stretched across the floor. Willing my tendons, muscles and joints to relax and reset. The chamber was small and just another prison cell. Three of the walls were brick, darkened with age and unidentified stains. The floor was bare concrete and decorated by a threadbare red rug, on the right there was a patched up double sofa, on the left a wooden desk and stool. Directly in front of me was a glass wall with a food slot and ventilation holes. Above me, hanging from a short chain was a light with an elegant shade, thankfully, it wasn't bright, more urine-stain yellow than white.

"I have been upgraded," I rasped and started at the sound of my voice.

Oh, my Gods, I thought with horror. I had never given much value to the sound of my voice - it was just something that came out of my face. It wasn't just rough; my voice was as broken and stitched as Why.

I chuckled and sprang up suddenly and stood in front of the glass wall and said, "Hello, Clarice."

11.

I was using my reflection in the glass wall to straighten my tie when a single light on the other side switched on and revealed The Rabbit standing under it.

For a moment we faced off in silence. His very blue eyes glaring at me from behind the rabbit face, his snow plough jaw set in such a fashion that it looked capable of denting an anvil. After long enough I sighed and sat in the double sofa. It was so dented and threadbare I could only guess how many hundreds of asses it had supported over the years.

"I'm curious how many different styles of dungeons the Queen actually has." I said.

"She is a nymphomaniac with a precarious grip on reality," The Rabbit said. Quickly checking his pocket watch before slipping it back into his waistcoat pocket, "She has one for every one of her odd little tastes. There is a catalogue available if you'd like to see it?"

I waved a hand, "Not necessary."

"Your voice seems... different," he commented.

I swallowed hard; it hurt, "Yes. Would it be a lot to ask for a glass of water?"

"Would you trust to drink any liquids we gave you?" The Rabbit asked inclining his head inquisitively, illustrated well with his long ears.

"Good point," I conceded.

"Anyway, from what we can tell you don't need to drink. Or to eat or even sleep, do you?"

Clearly, it was a rhetorical question. When I didn't answer he smiled, it was a pleasant smile, a strong smile even with the Halloween mask. He said, "I want to go home, Donnie. I want to leave this place."

"I'm sure you do, but it's all just a little bit unfair. Isn't it, Adam?" I said.

He lifted his significant chin and his posture went very slightly rigid at the mention of the name, "How did you know?"

I chuckled, which felt like barbwire in my oesophagus, "I am a detective," I said, "Back in Norwich."

"I thought you were an Ambassador?" he said.

"Titles," I said with a shrug, "The difference is mute. You are Adam, the First Man created by God…"

He acknowledged it with a single nod. He knew the game we played, so he was being courteous, it was something I fully planned to milk.

"Eve was created for you, why do you want to leave?"

Adam put a gloved hand onto the glass, "God has forgotten us now. We are a game that He has lost interest in playing. But despite this our game continues and it is one that is laced with irony. Eve was created for me after Lilith left and created so as not to repeat the errors that my first woman made."

"Errors?" I asked.

He sighed, resigning himself to the fact he would need to open himself up to me. It must have felt awful for him to do so, to realise he had to bare part of his internal dialogue to me, a lowly Nooseman. As lowly as they come but his only hope.

"Lilith was very headstrong from the start. Strong too, like me and to be honest the sex was just better with her."

I was about to comment on that point but bit my tongue and clapped a hand over my mouth to allow him to continue.

"Lilith was willing to try things; she wanted to explore and be explored. It was all physical, sexual, passionate. But she didn't want to be mounted, she refused, and I didn't like that. God said that Lilith's passion for the physical pleasure was an error. So, he made Eve... are you laughing?"

My hand squeezing my mouth shut I shook my head vigorously.

"Do you wish me to continue?" he asked snottily.

"Yes, I'm sorry, please do. We only have a page or two for this," I said.

"Eve was compassionate and soft from the beginning..."

"Sounds like you were too." I said, before I could stop myself. I immediately help up a contrite hand and said, "I'm sorry. Carry on please."

"...but this also meant she believed in the best of people and was easily manipulated. After Lilith was expelled, she met the Devil and together they hatched a plan to get myself and Eve expelled from paradise... no point going into details, as you know it worked pretty well. It was a lesson that we learnt, about the fragility of innocence and how certain lessons are learnt only after they leave scars. Eve was like a fine crystal glass, after being dismissed, it shattered her and while she didn't fall apart, the cracks run deep. She sees her old innocence as an embarrassing weakness and has devoted herself to being a deviant."

"You don't read that in the Bible," I mentioned.

"How else do you think we produced all of mankind?" he asked.

"I thought evolution had something to do with it?"

"Maybe it does. If we're all just characters in God's game, then origin stories and backgrounds can be rewritten to suit whoever is being played. Have you ever considered that maybe God isn't all powerful? But is merely a teenager sitting in his room at his parent's house occasionally playing a game that is created by someone else. Maybe our God isn't the creator at all, just the person who has his thumb on the shut-down key."

I held up a hand, finger splayed to stop him, "I'm sorry Adam, you have been torturing me for days, so please let us not get existential just yet. I beg you, get to the fucking point."

He took his hand away from the glass and straightened up in a huff, "Eve has changed."

"All wives do." I told him.

"She will let me go if you take my place," he said, "This means I can go back to Lilith."

I tried to laugh, it came out as a raspy melody of hiccups, "You think Lilith wants you out of Wonderland because she misses you?"

Adam spread his hands, "She can kill me for all I care. I will be free of Eve. Free of being a slave. Of being a servant."

"And in return I become a slave and a servant?" I pointed out.

"But you are accustomed to it," he said, "I have only been in this role since you were last here. That is a summation of a couple of years whereas you've been a slave to your noose for much longer."

"You're right," I said, standing up and wagging a finger, "The best thing to do is become a double slave, isn't it?"

"I don't appreciate sarcasm," he said, "Especially not from something of your level."

"Sorry *Mister* Rabbit," I grunted, "I'm not going to stay in Wonderland for you, I am going to find my way out of here, one way or another."

The Rabbit checked his pocket watch again and said, "I am sorry you are so inflexible on this."

"I have made up my mind," I said, "I do not belong in Wonderland."

He put his hands behind his back and his jaw moved as if he chewed on a thought, he turned on his heel and walked away from the glass, slipping out of the corridor light. His voice trailed behind him, "Nobody belongs in Wonderland," he said, "Why else do you think we are forced to resort to such madness?"

"What do you mean by that?" I asked the shadows beyond the glass, "It's not like you have me over a barrel is it?"

More lights were turned on, revealing that it wasn't a corridor beyond my cell but yet another chamber in the basements of the castle. The details of this room were lost though for what was featured only ten feet or so away from the glass.

"Me and my big mouth." I croaked.

Alice was trussed up over a barrel. Naked save for her red hood and cape her hands were fastened with ropes around the edge of the barrel and the same ropes wrapped around the circumference of the barrel and tied several ties around her knees, which in turn were spread. Her skin was untouched, not a bruise or a blemish. I was disappointed with myself that a part of me relished the sight of her voluptuous curves spread over a barrel - it was a momentary feeling as I recalled sourly that this woman had betrayed me.

"What is this?" I asked.

The Rabbit walked back into the light and said, "Plan B," he said, "I am straight up going to threaten you until you accept to drink all of the elixir."

"But I threw it away," I said.

"The Queen has been busy making more," he said.

I cringed and even Alice's face pinched in distaste, she snarled loudly, "When I get out of this, I'm going to hurt you, bunny boy!"

"Shut up," The Rabbit grunted, then to me he said, "And yes, you did spill all of the elixir. But it didn't go to waste."

A door off to the left beyond my line of vision opened, pouring in some new light in the shape of a long rectangle. There was a rattling of chains and the sounds of people struggling against something very strong.

The Rabbit strode over to the glass again and tapped it with a finger, "You know all those secret desires and fanciful whims that people keep hidden? Those animal desires that we don't succumb to because we know that the repercussions would be too severe to warrant them? But then," with the same tapping finger he pointed towards the light source, "You get that special nudge in the wrong direction and suddenly you can do nothing else but act on those instincts."

I tried to see what he was pointing to, when I couldn't, I looked at Alice, "Alice, what is it?"
But she was trussed up in such a fashion that she couldn't see past her shoulder; her eyes were wide and fierce, "I don't know, I can't see! Are you going to do something or not?!"

I spread my arms, "What can I do? I'm in prison!"
The Rabbit gave that smile again, "Just a nudge... sometimes it's a mistimed word, an unfortunate act of desperation... or some idiot spilling a bathtub full of aphrodisiacal ejaculate down a drain."
Alice and my eyes met as a realization dawned on both of us.
It played out quickly in my mind's eye, Kaben had been taken out of the castle but, obsessed with saving me, had found his way back. He must have met a host of obstacles and monsters along his way, but he was the sort of creature that such things would only motivate him further. He had climbed his way up the walls of the castle, entering via the only part of a castle that is always left unguarded no matter what castle it is. The arse hole. I could imagine the wolf man, eyes focused and enraged with his urge to settle his debt and save

me as he clambered through the plumbing of the castle, finally coming to a strategic position, ideally located and unprotected. That howling had echoed through the pipes that connected all the rooms of the castle, had been carried to every ear. A brilliant tactic to elude and terrify the enemy, he must have been ready to exact the last stage of his rescue just at the point when I poured an entire bathtub of the Queen's cum onto his head.

Alice started to struggle against the bonds while The Rabbit chuckled to himself and gestured to whoever was controlling Kaben to bring the wolf man into the room.

The Big Bad Wolf, was muzzled and bound with chains and leathers straps around his bulging chest, biceps and thighs, his heaving caused his fur to bristle up and down his body. His bloodshot eyes were wild, and foam fell from his maws but that wasn't the terrifying part. That was located lower down on his body, extending out of a furry curtain of ragged hair.

"Adam!" I shouted at the Rabbit, "Don't do this!"

"Will you drink the elixir?" he asked.

"Yes," I said, "Yes, yes I will."

"Good," he said, "But I'm going to do this to Alice and if you don't drink, I'm going to do the same thing to Cheshire and then anyone else we can get from your world into here."

I screamed a long line of unintelligible, raspy curses and threats at him while hurling myself against the glass wall but all I managed to do was bounce off of it.

"Donnie, you better do something quickly!" Alice said with amazing calmness as she tried to move but her position over the barrel hampered her, she could only wiggle slightly. The part she could wriggle did not help the situation.

"Adam," I shouted, "You stop this. You stop this now!"

But The Rabbit waved a dismissive hand at me and beckoned the guards bring Kaben forward. The wolf man spotted Alice in her prostrated position and his phallus swelled so visibly that the guards holding his bonds took quick steps away.

I pounded on the glass with my fist while Alice struggled to get free and The Rabbit watched with his own bulge in his pants. I noticed this last thing and felt my anger boil even further up my spine. The beast inside me began shaking at the cage in my head.

"Release him," The Rabbit said.

One of the guards, who I recognized from earlier, reached behind the quivering Kaben and pulled a chorded device that caused the leather straps and chains to unfasten and Kaben, with a roar exploded from them. Backhanding the guard so hard that his jar head shattered, and his half head hit the wall like a jelly fish.

In a single bound Kaben was upon Alice.

I didn't take my eyes away, not wanting to be the coward who had to look but I wish I had done. The full weight of the Big Bad Wolf landed upon Alice propelling the thrust of his hips and upon receiving it all her head arched upwards, her eyes as wide as her mouth, her wholebody tensing but unable to make a sound. The force he landed was with such bestial brutality that even The Rabbit stepped back away from it as if to avoid being collateral and the barrel she was strapped over cracked at its seams.

I continued to try and break through the glass until my arms were numb; I couldn't stomach watching this spectacle without acting against it. The wolf barked on every thrust that was powered it seemed by every muscle in his body. Spittle flew out from the muzzle he wore and dripped onto her back which was curved against his clawed paws that were gripping her around her midsection pulling her back against each of his thrusts. Kaben looked more human than animal, but this did not make the scene any more tolerable. It was impossible not to see the size of the weapon he was ploughing into her, the unsettling animal purple-red shine to it.

Finally, she found her breath and began making sounds. Unable to fight against it she recoiled from every thrust that must have been violently impaling her. They were the victim gasps someone makes with pain, airy, throaty sounds that carried over the creaking of the barrel.

"Kaben!" I shouted through the glass, turning and grabbing the furniture I could find and shattering it against the glass wall, "Kaben! Stop this! That is your Mistress!"

Against the violation Alice's hands screwed into fists and held onto her bonds, and her eyes were squeezed shut against it all, her lips drawn back away from her teeth to the extent I could see her gums. It was a face that made me think of bearing a terrible burning, the way that when burnt the pain doesn't decrease but only increases.

"Adam! I'm going to kill you for this!" I screamed picking up a piece of the bed frame and using it like a baseball bat to smash against the glass.
Moving faster than I could see him, The Rabbit appeared at the glass with both gloved hands flat pressed against it, leaning in he said in a low voice, "You watch closely Detective... this same fate will happen to Cheshire, if you try it. Then after Cheshire I'll personally locate your friends from above. Your assistant Danielle or perhaps your friend Nikita? Shall I go on? This," he pointed behind him, "Is just evidence for you that I do not bluff. Drink the Queen's elixir or I swear to you I will have you watch everyone you love and care for suffer the same fate and each of them will know that you are fully to blame because of your cowardly selfishness. How much suffering can you handle? How many women will you hear crying in pain and...?"

Only half way through his speech he noticed at about the same time as I did that something had changed with Alice. Not with Kaben, because he hadn't stopped, or changed, he was pulling her into every one of his thrusts as if he wanted to split her in half. The change was in Alice's vocalizations. Transforming from the painful, involuntarily gasps of pain they were now more akin to crooning sighs of pleasure. The difference of which were particularly significant, and The Rabbit looked over his shoulder in surprise.

I was dumbstruck, he was dumbstruck. The guards standing out of the way were dumbstruck, but of course they had no jaws to hang open. It was a weird moment, a moment perfectly suited to the basement of Hell.

"Err," The Rabbit said to me.

Her head still turned up, her eyes were still screwed shut, her lips still drawn back but now curled up at the corners in a heathen smile that suggested that the pain/pleasure ratio was shifting and there was no way to deny that she was, on each of Kaben's manic thrusts, pushing back as much as she could to meet them.

I cleared my throat loudly, "Um, Alice?"

She answered me by opening her eyes briefly to look in my way but her head swooned as she was rocked by another thrust that stole away whatever she was going to say, turning it into a shrill gasp that escaped through a heathen grin.

The Rabbit looked at me in confusion and I shrugged in response. We both looked at the guards, but they merely blinked and as one unit shrugged.

"This, was... um... unexpected," The Rabbit said, clearly not in the territory he had anticipated, "I won't lie, I don't really know what to do now."

I had turned away by this point and covering my ears humming, "Baby.... Baby... baby..."

"Mister! – *oh*- Rabbit!" Alice cried.

She was staring at the tall man as Kaben had shifted his position and was now gripping the barrel on both sides of Alice's head, his claws splintering the wood as he thrust with the added force of his arms.

"Yes?" The Rabbit asked.

I lingered at the far side of the cell, not really sure if I wanted to be closer to what was about to happen, I looked back as The Rabbit approached her to stand a little distance in front of the couple. While I felt sullied for watching this, The Rabbit was still clearly aroused. Alice's eyes were fixated on that part of him.

"Take it- *oh bugger right there!* – out!" she commanded.

This wasn't happening. This wasn't happening. I thought to myself, I was still being tortured and was just hallucinating! I crouched by the far wall. Alice had used that authorative voice that no man is able to disobey. Unbuckling his belt and his trousers, his erection, easily as large as the Big Bad Wolf's, sprung out of his pants to such an attention it shook. He took his member in his hand and with a casual confidence kicked away his trousers and stepped forward, having to crouch a little to allow Alice to take him into her mouth.

A new chorus of sounds emanated from them and I closed my eyes and chanted louder, "Baby...baby...baby...ohh!" with abandon, wanting to drown out what was happening in front of me.

I was chanting it for the seventh time when a pair of hands touched my shoulders and a voice said in my ear, "Be ready."

Springing up in fear I spun in a full circle but was alone in the cell. I looked at the scene and a lot of stuff happened suddenly and all at once.

Kaben started growling heavily as he approached his climax. At the same time, his claws splintered the barrel into parts, releasing Alice's bonds.

Simultaneously, Cheshire exploded into presence right above The Rabbit's face, her thighs catching him around the neck and her crotch mashing against his face. He staggered backwards and slipped out of Alice's mouth with a pop. Cheshire rode The Rabbit's head down to the ground while Alice was overcome with a climatic orgasm of such dizzying proportions that she squeezed herself clean off of Kaben's enraged member and went flying forward like a rocket trailing ropes, bits of barrel and a long line of thick, milky stuff colliding with Cheshire like a flying rugby player. The pair of them sailed over The Rabbit, who even when caught by surprise, was still silly fast. He whipped around and tried to grab them, but the pair vanished in a poof.

    At the exact same moment, the guards, who were quicker on the uptake, had already fled the room and locked the door behind them. The big locking bolt clanked into place just as Kaben, swollen like a balloon and imminently climaxing, spotted the only other available hole in the room.

    An explosion of purple smoke surrounded me, and Cheshire appeared at my side, grabbed hold of me, and we left the cell. But not before I saw Kaben lunge for The Rabbit and just after I heard a tearing sound that would linger in my memory almost as long as the horrified scream that accompanied it.

12.

"I think I'm going to throw up," I said, sitting down on one of the mushrooms along the side of the lane.

Cheshire took off her coat and put it around Alice's shoulders, and pinched her chin between her thumb and forefinger, "You okay, Red?"

Alice smiled and nodded.

"I am very lost," I said to them, "Since when are the two of you friends?"

The pair of them exchanged a glance, it was Cheshire who explained, "We've been planning to get you out of prison for a long time. But we had to wait for the right moment and the right opportunity."

I clasped both hands together in an expression of pleading, "I've had a lot to take in so please forgive me if I'm a little slow on the uptake. You planned all of that?"

"No," Alice said, limping over, "Not all of that. But we knew the opportunity would come and we would just have to improvise."

"But you... and Kaben... you planned that?"

Alice blushed, "I have been his mistress for a long time, so he doesn't scare me."

I recoiled a little from her then, "But he's a dog!"

"Wolf actually," she said, "And he's half human so there's nothing wrong with it."

"You've had sex with me," Cheshire pointed out, standing with her arms crossed, heavy judgement shining at me from under the rim of her hat.

I opened my mouth to say something, closed it, thought of something else to say, gave up on that and instead put my face in my hands.

"How long was I in prison for?"

"Six months," Alice told me, "What did they do to you?"

They both paled when I told them.

"That's inhuman," Cheshire muttered.

"Bastards," Alice said.

"So, Alice," I said, carefully choosing my words, "Is Kaben going to kill The Rabbit?"

"Hopefully not," the bounty hunter said with a cruel smile, "That Rabbit has been pumping him full of elixir for the whole time you've been in prison. Ever since you poured it all over him and he got hold of the Tweedle brothers."

"Oh, my god no,"

"And Benny," Cheshire said.

"He... with Benny?"

Cheshire and Alice nodded together, and I didn't press the matter but asked an important question of what was next.

"Cheshire is coming with us when we leave Wonderland," Alice said.

"What about your powers?" I asked.

"I won't have them anymore," Cheshire said, "But it's a hit I'm willing to take."

"And we're not leaving without Kaben," Alice added.

"Okay," I said, "Then why doesn't Cheshire just pop in and poof him out?"

"Do you want to try to handle him as he is now?" Alice asked.

I really, *really* didn't. I asked, "What will it take for him to calm down?"

"I think he has to work it out of his system," Alice explained, "Fortunately, Cheshire has bribed the guards and they won't be opening the dungeon until either we tell them too or the Queen does. And, since Adam is immortal, Kaben will be able to work the elixir out of his system."

"That's a polite way of putting it," I said.

The cat handed my knob over and said, "It's the way of the world, Donnie. Saving you has made this a bit more complicated; the Queen of Hats now knows that my allegiance is with you, she will be furious at what's been done to The Rabbit and she'll be wanting our blood."

"Eve is immortal though," I said, "What do you propose?"

"We replace The Rabbit," Alice said.

"I'm not doing it," I said.

"Of course, you aren't, we need you to get us out of Wonderland," Cheshire said, "But I'm sure we can find a replacement somewhere."

I thought we could, I stood up and said, "Thank you for taking that hit for me Alice,"

"No problem," she said, "I really need a cigarette. Ever notice how much you want to smoke after a massive orgasm?"

I cringed and Cheshire thumped me in the shoulder.

Beyond the trees, somewhere upwards, there was a horrible sound that was lightly familiar but awful to behold.

"What was that?" I asked.

"I think that was Benny," Cheshire said.

Like a ragged shadow the monster that was previously Benny The Caterpillar exploded from above the trees screeching like a banshee out of hell. As dark as the sky above it I perceived only wide ragged wings, a long neck and a vicious whip-like tail. It must not have seen us because it flew over us without stopping but Cheshire grabbed us and we vanished in a cloud and reappeared deep in the forest under some ferns the size as a house.

"I thought Benny had been shagged to death?" I said, somewhat accusingly, I had been relieved to hear that monstrous Bobbit-worm-caterpillar from Hell was dead.

"What do Caterpillars turn into, Donnie?" Alice asked.

I pointed at the direction of that screaming wailing monstrosity, "That's not a butterfly!"

"No, it's a dragon," Cheshire said, "Bobbit Caterpillars turn into dragons Donnie."

I sat down again my head in my hands.

Standing around me I heard the girls talking again. I got the feeling that they were innovating as they went along, the plan being pretty much to get me out of the castle. Now, the fact that Kaben was trapped in the castle presented us with a new complication, but a better one all things considered because at least I was out of the dungeon and had my knob in hand. Also, as a matter of perspective Kaben was stuck in the castle but everyone in the castle was stuck in there with him too.

We had to act fast.

"Do you know of a lake nearby?" I asked.

13.

"How do you know that this is going to work?" Cheshire asked.

"Like Alice said, Kaben is half man but also half wolf, the principle remains the same," I said, "But if you have a better idea, you're welcome to suggest something."

The cat didn't have anything to suggest, neither did the hood, it turned out that both of them considered the success of their last daring rescue to be mostly good fortune and incredible luck.

I referred to the diagram I had drawn in the dirt at the side of the lane, illuminated by one of the glowing mushrooms; it showed a neat illustration of how we were going to save the day.

"You're going to have your head cut off," Cheshire said bluntly.

"Nobody ever trusts me," I muttered, "Adam says he wants to leave but he can't until he has a replacement. He wasn't able to say it at the time, but I believe that the Rabbit's mask is controlling him and that The Queen is controlling him through her Hat."

"If that was true why would he be able to tell you everything he did?" Alice asked. She was sitting awkwardly on the mushroom top as her legs were still shaking.

"Not all control is conscious, maybe it just stops him from leaving but either way he can't take it off. I'm sure he would have done by now because he looks ridiculous," I went over the plan again, "So Cheshire, firstly, you get me into the Queen's chamber- I take her hat off, when I've done that you jump into the dungeon, snatch Kaben and drop him into the lake. The middle of it would be better and the colder the better. Alice will be waiting at the lake shore to make sure he doesn't go mental when he gets out of the water. By that time the hat will be off the Queen and you can grab Adam. Bring him to Alice and Kaben and then all of you head to the hotel."

"What about you?" Cheshire asked.

"What about Harold?" Alice asked.

"I'm sure that if you're planning on leaving Harold will let you go. Either way, he's the least of my concerns right now. Take my knob with you just in case I'm caught again. Once you're at the hotel safely stay there and wait for me. Agreed?"

"Agreed,"

It was a terrible plan.
Cheshire was right, it was probably going to get my head cut off and I'd be stuck serving the Queen as a fishbowl jar head guard. But it was the best plan we had, and I had survived dumber ideas so it was with this uneasy confidence that I took Cheshire's hand and vanished from the relative safety of the lane and reappeared in the main chamber of the castle.

On hindsight Cheshire probably chose the particular spot that she did so that I would almost certainly catch the Queen off guard. I would have preferred somewhere more tactical, like behind the throne or maybe perched upon one of the curtain railings, but instead she chose ten feet directly above the Queen's bloody hat.

Dropping the ten feet with stealthy ninja silence, I crashed upon the hat with all of my weight, slamming the entire thing down upon the Queen's head until it thumped against her shoulders. I bounced off the throne, landing nimbly on the throne stairs and leapt with at the nearest guard with a *nidan geri*, or double-footed jump kick. My heels smashed into his jar head, not breaking the glass but rattling what was left of his head inside the bowl and this allowed me the chance to grab the halberd he carried with the wicked, head-removing blade at the top of it.

The Queen of Hats, from inside her hat was bellowing commands while trying to get the hat off her whole head, she stood up, missed the first step to her throne and took a tumble.

Of the twenty-seven guards I had counted on my ten-foot drop, five of them turned their backs on me to help her and lost their jars for their efforts. The Queen staggered to her feet and slipped on one of their decapitated half heads.

Meanwhile, I demonstrated the effects of a childhood of forced instruction in the art of bojutsu, and how easy it is to gain impressive momentum when you keep the battle axe blade at an end of a long shaft spinning around your body. Glass jars shattered and wet, decomposing heads flew left, right and centre.

I shifted my moves from the crazy, arching spins to a lower stance as fewer guards meant more area for them to avoid the spinning end of my weapon. This allowed me to tie them up, throw them off balance when they attacked and send them staggering into each other like idiots.

One of them got lucky and struck me through the chest with a sword but it didn't stop me from shattering his jar with a high-wielding *muwashi geri* round house kick and then dropping the halberd for the sword itself.

I am better with shorter weapons anyway and this meant for the stronger eight that remained I went for their legs, rolling between them and striking at the steam junction joints that they relied on to stand. This made them bundle up and run clumsily into each other which made it easier to take out their jars.

It wasn't clean; by the end of it I looked like a pin cushion and was rattling with the number of swords sticking out of my torso but aside from that I felt pretty satisfied with how things were going.

"You're such a dick Donnie!" The Queen of Hats bellowed from where she stood in front of the steps to the throne. The Hat back atop her head, it was steaming, and the machine parts were whirling a bit more than they had before, emphasizing her anger.

I bowed; the blades sticking out of my back rattled, "I take that as a compliment, your Majesty," I said.

She unbuckled her robe and let it fall around her feet, she now stood naked save for the blazing red tattoos, the face paint and the oversized hat, I gave her a winning smile, "It's actually funny. I really wouldn't have minded shagging you."

"Oh, you'll see that opportunity yet," she promised.

"Take off the hat," I said, pointing the sword in my hand at her.

She ran at me with alarming speed scooping up one of the downed spears in her stride, hefting it up and throwing it at me like a javelin. I slipped to the side just in time, as the spear passed so close to me that it sliced through my tie knot and smashed a hole through the chamber doors behind me. When I faced her again, she kicked me with the blade of her foot and the full extension of her lengthy leg and I smashed through the same doors, leaving the blades and weapons that had been in me, clattering to the floor at her feet.

There was a crash of guards beyond the door as, lucky for me, I collided with one of the first ones approaching on the way out of the chamber and knocked them all down like dominoes. I re-entered the chamber carrying an axe and screaming like a savage.
The axe snapped across her forearm and while I managed to avoid two out of three of her attacks, the ones that she tagged me with counted for a lot.

"I would have enjoyed seeing you as my Rabbit," she heaved, "You would have been a fighter, despite how small you are, Nooseman!"

"You know I'm pretty well hung," I hissed, blocking one of her punches and delivering a dirty shot, a donkey kick to her lower abdomen, she choked and bent double and like an idiot I went, "Boom! Right in the ovar- *ooffff!*"
I crashed into the throne twenty feet away, clutching at myself. She wiped her hands together and retorted, "Boom, right in the nuts."

Guards were pouring into the chamber now. They poured in and encircled me in a bull horns formation, but they wouldn't attack until the Queen gave the command.

"So Cheshire got you out of your cell?" The Queen said, walking towards me, her hat making a rattling noise and shooting out more steam than usual, "I will have to have some particular words with her about that."

"And where's your Rabbit?" I wheezed, my nuts hurt so bad I was afraid to move from where I lay on the throne, even my hoarse whisper was high-pitched, "I would have liked to have words with him. Shouldn't your man help fight your battles?"

"I don't need him to fight my battles for me," she said, kicking aside one of the guards' robotic shells as if it were a pillow in her way, she started climbing the stairs. Her hat was really making quite a racket now and it looked like it was vibrating on her head, "I am not a weak or cowering woman who can be easily deceived."

She stood over the throne now and leaned over me, her face directly in front of mine, her thick curls blocking out the rest of the room, the hat kicking up a storm above us. She looked at the copious blood on my shirt and, as if testing the legitimacy of the wound, pushed her finger into one of the holes. I jerked.

"This is impressive, you can't die but you can scar and bleed," she unbuttoned my shirt and drew it open to look at my wounds, "Oh, these scars, I could have had so much fun learning about them."

"You don't have to bleed to leave scars," I said, "Do you know where your Rabbit is?"

"Probably wondering where you've disappeared to," she asked, "He is so gullible, he always has been."

"Do you know where the Big Bad Wolf is?" I asked as she traced the line that one of the halberds had made as it sliced through four ribs at the front and at least six on the back, transfixed by how they were already knitting together. She shook her head.

I started to chuckle. The chuckle became a full-on laugh and the laugh became hysterical.

"What are you laughing at?" she asked.

I couldn't stop laughing, it was maddening, and I clutched at my sides, gagging while at the same time giggling, chortling and howling with laughter.

"Why are you laughing?" she shouted, slapping me hard and when that didn't stop me, she grabbed me by the throat and heaved me off the throne and held me aloft, my shoes dangling above the throne steps, "Tell me why you are laughing?"

I took hold of her wrist with my hands, to alleviate the grip on my throat as I looked her in the eyes and told her where her dear Rabbit probably was right now.

She swore at me in some ancient language which I had once heard Lilith swear at me in, I took that moment to act and leveraged the grip I had on her wrist jammed two fingers into her eyes and flicked the hat off her head. It went over backwards, toppling to the floor and taking with it her golden hair and the better part of her scalp, leaving Eve standing there with a very annoyed look on her face and only half a head.

Instead of brain matter and a skull there were metal plates, whirling gyros and moving gears, things clicked, ticked and whirled.

"You annoy me," she said, thrusting me back into the throne so that it rocked onto its hind legs. She reached up to the machinery part of her skull and the top of it opened up and from it she withdrew a small package, wrapped in brown paper and tied with string.
I was surprised that I could still be surprised. She opened the package and revealed a biscuit which she bit into, "You ready for this?" she asked, chewing.

"Probably not,"
The Queen closed her eyes and cried out as in a spectacular fashion she doubled in size, then within the same second, quadrupled in size. The throne was pushed over backwards as she loomed, bigger and bigger and I rode it backwards as it was pushed by the accelerated expansion of her big toe. Soon she was towering over me, head up in the rafters, her face manic; when she spoke, it thrummed through the chamber and shattered the glass jars of all of her guards at once, "Now!" the giant Queen roared, "You fuck me!"

She reached down for me but this time at least I was quick on the uptake and I leapt from the throne and sprinted down the stairs and across the room, sprinting behind the pillars and hurdling the guards in my way to put as many obstacles behind us as possible.
Cheshire poofed out of a cloud alongside me and said, "What the blazes is taking you so long?!"

"Change of plan!"

The Queen lunged for me, her gigantic car-sized hand enclosing around Cheshire instead but when her fingers clasped shut all they got was smoke. I skidded to a stop outside the chamber and backed up against the wall. Cheshire appeared beside me, "Where is Kaben?"

"He's still shagging the Rabbit," she said, "We were waiting for you to give the signal!"

"Was I meant to give a signal?!"

The Queen's shoulder hit the wall behind me hard and her arm shot out of the doors, sweeping across the floor trying to grab me. I threw myself bodily down the spiral staircase to avoid her gigantic hand and it felt like I hit every single step on the way down.

On my back at the bottom of the stairs Cheshire appeared above me, and I said in a strained voice, "Signal given please continue the plan."

She burst into a cloud.

And reappeared a second later with The Rabbit, she dropped him onto the floor in front of me and I recoiled in horror, "What did Kaben do to his face?"

"We have a problem," she said.

The Rabbit no longer wore the mask, but not only did he lack the upper face of a rabbit, but he lacked most of that face at all. The mask had not only dissolved but replaced the bone of his entire upper skull. From the nose and all the way around was neatly sawn off, revealing only brain and eyeballs dangling from the optic nerves and various muscles. That was bad enough and the smell was considerably worse but it was that the poor creature was still alive that terrified me.

I kicked away from him until I was backed up against the wall. Cheshire floated next to me, "He is not the problem though,"

"What do you mean?" I asked.

"The mask is now on Kaben,"

"*Mistress,*" Adam, The former Rabbit, groaned, "*Rabbit, needs... mistress.*"

"Is he okay?" I asked Cheshire.

"Television is out of the question," she said.

"I meant Kaben,"

"He scared the crap out of me," Cheshire said, "But I dropped him into the lake as you said. What do we do now?"

I was already on my feet and running to the chamber where the Queen was shaking the castle to its foundations, "Getting that hat!"

Half way up the stairs Cheshire grabbed me around the waist muttering, "You only have to bloody well ask," and we went from the staircase to the chamber where, still in mid stride I tripped over one of the fallen guards on my way to the hat and went tumbling across the carpet. I saw the hat sitting at the foot of the stairs, bouncing along as its mechanisms whirled and clicked and burred; right next to it, having been discarded in all the swelling and growing, was the remaining bit of biscuit that the Queen, still on her hands and knees at the door trying to dig her way out of the chamber to get to me, had eaten.

Cheshire picked up the Hat and held it with her arms outstretched and I picked up the bit of biscuit.

"What's that?" she asked.

"This is a terrible idea," I said, "Get Adam."

One poof gone, another poof back, this time with the groaning lump that was Adam and I quickly explained what I wanted to do. Cheshire looked genuinely appalled.

"I don't want to go there," she moaned.

"Just do it," I commanded.

I got Adam to his feet, easily avoiding the gaze of his eyeballs as they bounced upon the ends of his shoelace-optic nerves. Cheshire flew away to the nearby wall so that she could get a run up and when she was ready, I stuck the biscuit bit into Adam's mouth. Cheshire collided with him and the pair of them vanished and reappeared somewhere else in the chamber.

What followed was very unpleasant and has been omitted in case my mother ever gets to read this book. So, considering what has happened so far you can imagine what happened.

Cheshire could appear and reappear anywhere in Wonderland assuming the space was big enough to fit. One space was, temporarily, big enough to fit Adam.

The Queen gasped in surprise as Adam appeared somewhere, she had not expected, "What is go- " she began but by that time the biscuit had started to work and Cheshire grabbed me and the hat and took us out of there before things got very, very unpleasant.

14.

Alice was waiting on the shoreline for Kaben when we appeared next to her, her hands clasped in front of her chest the concern on her face for the wolf man was touching.

"Is that The Hat?" she asked, taking a step away from it when I presented it to her.

"Yes, but you might need it," I said but didn't have time to explain when Kaben surfaced from the water, The Rabbit's mask on his face minus one half an ear. He roared and charged.

Cheshire leapt in front of the wolf man to try and stop him, but he swung at her with one arm and looked like he smashed her to smoke before he continued charging down on Alice. She snatched the hat out of my hands and pulled it onto her head. The machinery paused for a second, then there was a crunching sound and Alice staggered and fell. Kaben accelerated his charge at a terrifying speed and caught her in one of his huge paws.

"Are you alright Alice?" He asked in a voice that was his but not Kaben's.

The machinery around the hat started moving and ticking again, tendrils of steam coming out of the vents, "Yes," said Alice, "I am fine. Good to have you back."

Kaben grinned a big doggy grin, "Good to be back."

I remembered to exhale and dropped my hands. In a shrill whistle I spoke, "Is everything okay?"

Kaben made sure Alice was on her feet then straightened and faced me, "Very well, thanks to you and Cheshire."

The cat appeared behind me and said, "Is everything okay?"

"It's fine Cheshire," Alice said, "Things are as they should be."

In the distance, in the direction of the castle there was a sound of something massive and horrible happening, involving a great deal of screaming and destruction of property.

"Pretty much as it should be," Alice corrected herself, "Can we go?"

"No, hold on, are you guys sure you're alright?" I pressed.

Kaben answered, "I can't speak for Alice, but I've never felt so calm or so at ease."

"But the mask," I said, illustrating vaguely with my hands, "It really didn't agree with Adam, it ate into his skull."

The wolf man considered things for a reason, then reached up and with a little tug removed the Rabbit mask from his face. He looked okay beneath it; the fur of his face pressed down, but not injured. Pensively, he considering things for a moment.

"Without it I feel more animal than man," he said, "But I don't think it's very dangerous."

He handed it to me, and I turned it over in my hands. The inside of it had several components that I could identify and some other devices and mechanisms that I couldn't. There was nothing that should have spooked me and nothing that could have eaten into the skull of an immortal, but this didn't make me feel any better. Nevertheless, I offered it back to the wolf man and he held up a big hand, "I don't need it back right now," he said.

I tested its weight in my hands but didn't consider putting it on my face, I referred to Alice, "What about your Hat?"

"I'm not sure," she said. But reached up above her and with both hands pulled it up without any difficulty, she handed the Hat over and Cheshire took it in both hands and held it out again as if expecting it to explode.

"No need to look so disappointed you two," Alice said to us. She looked at Kaben, "Do I have hat hair?"

The wolf man shook his head, "No, Mistress. Do you have my chain?"

"I'm afraid I don't have it anymore, Kaben," she said, "Do you need it?"

"Without the mask I feel a little less able to control myself," he admitted, "Even now I can feel my rage building up."

Cheshire peeked into the bowls of the Hat, "It doesn't seem dangerous... what do you think, Donnie?"

"Not sure," I admitted.

"Maybe sometimes bad things happen to bad people," Alice offered.

"Hmm, well, it's up to you," I said, "I won't lie this has been a bit of a humdinger of an adventure for me and I... well... I don't care. Do want them back?"

Kaben and Alice looked at each other and after some silent communication they agreed. I handed over the hat and the mask, frankly glad to be rid of them.

"You look better wearing a mask," I said to Kaben.

"If only we could get one for you now," he replied.

15.

Cheshire snuck us into the hotel room, but the subterfuge was unnecessary as with any disaster the destruction of the Queen's castle had the attention of all the staff of the hotel including Harold who stood out in the parking area watching as the castle was brought to its foundations. The rumbling sounds of falling stone and crashing timber echoing over the forest.

At the wall that we entered into I offered it the door knob and the door emerged out of the plaster work and as I pressed the device to it there was that reliable clinking and connecting of internal mechanics. I twisted it and brought open the way back to our home. I held the door open for them and said, "Home you go," I said.

"What do you mean?" Kaben asked, his mask reflecting more light in the darkened antechamber beyond the door than his fur did, turning him into a glowing rabbit's face eight feet up, "Aren't you coming?"

"I can't," I admitted, "Not yet. It's my fault all of this happened in the first place and I'm not going to leave here with giant Adam and Eve free to roam around. I have to bring them out of Wonderland, bring them both back."

Kaben ran a claw along the top of the door frame, "I do not think they will fit through here at the moment,"

"I can possibly help with that," Cheshire said, stepping in close embracing my arm supportively, "I would like to leave here without any regret."

"Adam is my bounty," Alice said, "I can stay as well."

"No," I said, "You and Kaben have the very things that gave them power, you need to get out of Wonderland more than you need to stay. When I bring them back the bounty is yours. Well, maybe you can give me a small cut,"

Kaben reached through the door and placed his hand on my shoulder, "Are you sure?"

I nodded, "Absolutely, look after her and get home safe. Now go."

The Big Bad Wolf nodded, ushered Alice into the antechamber and closed the door behind him. I removed the doorknob from the wall and slipped it into my pocket and watched the door recede from view.

Cheshire, still holding onto my arm said, "Where to now?"

"I know it is a lot to ask Cheshire," I said, "But this is one last favour I need to ask of you."

"Anything,"

"Will you take off your hat for me?"

The cat looked at me quizzically, "Whatever for?"

I disentangled my arm from her and put my hands into my pockets to show I meant her no harm, but asked again, "Please Cheshire, just take off your hat."

She frowned, backing away, "No. I'm not playing your game Donnie, I'm not going to do it."

"Why not?"

"Because you're being silly," she said.

"Is it because you can't take off the hat?" I pressed.

Like an animal caught in the corner her eyes were wide and snaking around, those wide cat slit irises searching for escape routes.

"You can't remove the hat because you are the real Queen of Hats, aren't you? It's your top hat that's got the real power, isn't it?"

"Please stop it Donnie, you scare me when you say such odd things," she pleaded.

"If I'm scaring you why don't you just disappear?" I asked, "Why don't you just poof away unless it's because you know that what I'm saying is the truth? Come on Cheshire, just take it off. Let me see what's under that hat."

I took a hand out of my pocket and slowly reached up towards the brim of her hat. It wasn't a big top hat; neither huge nor gregarious like the Queen's, this was small, compact; a lady's hat.

"You're mad," she whimpered, cringing away from my hand as it rose up passed her face.

"Oh, we are all quite mad, here aren't we?" I asked her.

The tips of my fingers touched the brim of her hat and her eyes were wide and focused on them, her irises vibrating gently as I applied a small amount of pressure to lift it from her head. Then I ceased, lowered my hand and stepped away from her.

"What are you playing at?" she asked, still cringing up against the wall.

I massaged my temples with my fingers and said, "Cheshire, I am sorry, I've had a very confusing time of things. That was rude of me to try and take your hat off you, please forgive me."
She took a shuddering breath, straightened herself up and regained some of her composure, "It's quite alright," she said, "Just scary."

I smiled, "As scary as the giant immortals we're going to be dealing with?"

"I am concerned about what we are going to find when we go there," she admitted.

"Either way, they need to be smaller to get through this door. You said you knew a way to help that?"

She crouched down and withdrew a small glass vial with a cork in it containing a very slightly pink liquid from her boot, "A drop of this potion will shrink them to normal size, give or take."

"You keep it in your boot?" I asked.

"A cat has to feel safe," she said, putting the vial into my hand, then with the other hand she reached up and pulled off her hat revealing that her thick purple hair was indeed suffering slightly from hat hair, "Just so we know we're on the same page."

"Thank you," I said, "But it was unnecessary. Can you take me to the castle?"

"In a poof," she said taking my hand.

Thick cloaks of dust hung over the ruined castle and it was eerily quiet for something that had seen so much destruction so quickly. We appeared in the great chamber, where I had faced the Queen. The grand ceiling had been demolished and lay in huge piles of rubble across the floor. The bodies of guards lay entangled amongst the rubble, the metal components so twisted that they barely resembled their former selves, the organic bits reduced to nothing but puddles of muck. The air was choking with dust so thick it swirled around us as we walked through it.

"Where are they?" Cheshire asked.

I held my finger to my lips and peered around in the gloom. Without the benefit of lamplights or a moon, the scant light that we did get from the soupy sky was barely enough to penetrate the dust let alone the darker shadows of the chamber.

"Could they have shrunk by themselves?" I said softly.

Cheshire shook her head and gently alighted into the air to drift casually behind me as I picked my way through the chamber walking over the fallen slabs of stone and mortar which had been crushed flat by heavy hands. At the end of the chamber, where there had been the doors, there was a huge hole that led down into the lower floors of the castle.

"Do you think they smashed their way all the way down to the foundations?" Cheshire asked.

It looked that way. I had no idea how many floors this castle had; I had seen so little of it during my tour of the dungeons. The hole must have been made and the remainder of the castle had fallen in, leaving only an outside shell of wall. The Castle had gone from a vast palace to an inhospitable pit in only a matter of hours. Because of me.

"Do you want to go there?" Cheshire said, crouching in mid-air and peering over my shoulder into the dark hole.

"Not particularly," I admitted, "Maybe we could get some kind of light down there, look around, see if there's anything we could use."

I sifted through the rubble, but it was too dark to see what was what. But a second later Cheshire returned with a lantern, a box of matches and a fire torch.

"How deep do you think this hole goes?" she asked.

Crouched over the lantern I opened up the cage and dipped the torch into the oil, first I lit up the lantern's candle and handed that to Cheshire who held it out like some kind of magical weapon against evil.

"Keep the light away from the hole," I said, lighting the torch and using it to navigate to the very edge of the chamber floor I tossed it into the abyss.

The firelight lit up the walls of the hole in brilliant orange flame as it fell down showing the scraggly remnants of the individual floors as it descended. It hit the bottom of the hole that was only seven floors distance beneath us.

"Not so deep," Cheshire said.

And then the bottom of the hole started to move, unfolding itself to reveal that it had been the curled-up body of the Queen herself. The fire light was snuffed out almost instantly as it was crushed beneath the folds of her skin as she moved; the sound she made as she did was horrible.

"Move it!" I shouted, turning and running back towards the far side of the chamber and clambering up the stairs and hiding behind the upturned thrones. Cheshire put the lamplight down in the centre of the chamber and poofed next to me where she crouched, shivering as the Queen climbed out of the hole passing into the lantern light.

"Where are you?" the Giant Queen boomed, her voice carrying and hurting our ears.
She slammed a hand down onto the chamber floor and stone slabs fell from the walls with a crash. When she hauled herself out of the hole it wasn't with the use of her legs which she dragged up behind her like a mermaid pulling up her tail.

Cheshire took a breath and I clapped a hand over her mouth to silence her and said into her ear, "I know, that's what we did. We can live with it later."
Adam had become part of Eve's body. The unnatural growth that the biscuits had produced had melded them together. Now Eve's torso bulged out to grotesque portions, her spine twisting visibly around the protruding bulge of a man's shoulder in her lower back and her legs were contorted and spread awkwardly around the abdomen of Adam, his legs dangling loosely like the forgotten limbs of some underdeveloped Siamese twin.

"Where are you?" she cried again, clawing through the rubble, she reached over, and her hand would have crushed us like ants if Cheshire hadn't poofed us to another vantage point slightly higher in the ruins of the castle where one of the towers had once been. It was above the Queen and out of reach, but it gave a better view point of the monstrosity we had caused.

"How can she live through this?" Cheshire asked me.

"She is immortal," I said, "She cannot die."

"And Adam?"

As if to answer this question Eve abruptly clutched at her body and cried out in pain as her guts contorted and bulged briefly in the shape of an elbow and a forearm, ending in a hand that pressed out against the skin of her stomach, just under the curve of her ribcage.

Cheshire started to hyperventilate, "He is still alive?" she squeaked.

"Do they need to ingest the potion for it to work?" I asked, but the cat wasn't listening, she was staring at the monster below us, her eyes wide and unblinking, her bottom lip quivering, "Cheshire!"

She shook her head a little, "No, they don't," she managed a hand on the stone remains of the stone wall in front of us to steady herself, "It just needs to be dropped onto them for it to work."

"Each of them or altogether?"

She didn't understand what I meant so I went in as blunt as possible, "I think that they have melded together- they are technically the same thing. They're no longer two people but the same thing."

"But he's conscious inside her," Cheshire said.

I leaned over and held her shoulders, "Listen to me," I said, "We can dwell on this later. But right now, I need to know how do I use this potion? Do I just drop it on them and hope for the best? Or do I need to serve it to them in a glass?"

"A drop will do," she said, "Don't give it all to them though if you want them to be back to normal,"

"Okay," I said, "Can you get me closer to them?"

No, that was what her expression said. No hell. No way. No chance. She was pinned to the stone she hid behind and too terrified to move. I said nothing else and started to climb down the tower as quietly as I could.

I didn't understand why the Giant Queen didn't extinguish the lantern. It was as if she wanted to be seen in the light, or maybe she didn't care to destroy it because she was in too much pain to notice it. I crept down from the tower along the crevices and the cracks of the walls, moving very slowly in an effort to conceal my approach. I paused regularly, bided my time, caught my breath and worked out an approach based on only a few steps ahead.

The closer I got, the more I could hear. The robotic parts of the Giant Queen's brain clanked and whirled as loud as a steam locomotion, pistons squealing in the night but that noise itself was drowned out by the rumbling, tremulous *inside* sides that were made whenever Adam tried to move inside.

Did Adam understand what was happening to him? Could he understand with that level of trauma to his face and god knew damage to his brain?

They could stay like that forever, the beast inside whispered, *Just think of the possibilities that await you.*

I shook my head and continued my way down.

Cheshire had relocated us to the other side of the hole and to get back to the throne side of the hole where the Giant Queen was sitting, I had to go down and around the outside where the damage to the castle was less severe and take a long route around.

This took me through the exterior gardens that were built directly onto the mountain that held the castle. It looked peaceful and beautiful: hedges shaped like animals and rose-bushes shaped like people. And it overlooked the landscape that was Wonderland.

It was a huge world. As compact and scrunched as Norwich, Wonderland, when folded out was an expansive world. From this high vantage point I saw seas and lands speckled with lit up cities. I had thought this world was isolated between the hotel and this castle. But there were populations of people here who even I had not affected yet. What were they doing now? Those fools sitting around their home fires across the waters, what were they thinking, saying and doing?

I couldn't linger and scaled the outside of the building, moving only half a foot each time and being highly selective of my footing and positioning. I came to a huge gash in the wall where a slab of stone had slid down and taken out an entire foundation leaving a gap large enough to sail a yacht through. I had nowhere to go aside from across it.

So, I leapt into the empty space, dropped twice as far as I went across but hit the other end with my full body and slid across jagged stone and mortar and rock until my searching hands found something of purchase and I came to a stop with my legs dangling over the edge.

Piece of cake, the beast grunted.

It took another half an hour to scale the remainder of the wall and when I climbed over the lip into the chamber, I rolled silently across the rubble strewn floor to hide behind a pillar.

The Queen Giant; Eve, was looking up at the sky and her face said it all. Tears the size of trash bags fell from her eyes and splashed onto the chamber floor and every one of her breaths was heavy. I watched her for half an hour as she cried, wiping her face with her hands. Adam moved inside her again and her face contorted in pain, her lips grimacing, revealing gaps where some of her teeth had been knocked out. Eve, the Mother of Man, was a broken woman. It's a look that you never forget, the look of a person who realizes that there is something horrible that will now define their lives and shape their future. That realization that the universe is not fair and that it doesn't care about your happiness… that sudden realization, that the truth of time and space is that we journey it alone.

I no longer had the stomach for this.

I called out from my hiding place, "Eve, can you hear me?"

She sniffed loudly but didn't strike. She didn't try to crush me or dig me out, she just looked around for the source of my voice, sniffed once again and said, "Donnie? I thought you had left," she said (her relief that I was there made me feel despicable), "I can hear you."

"Eve, I don't want to fight you anymore, I don't like what I did to you and Adam. I want to fix things if I can."

"What can you do, Nooseman?" she grunted, then laughed, "This is what I'm stuck with. God has completely forsaken me now."

"I can take you out of Wonderland," I said, "Take you to a place where they can offer you help. There are things that can be done to reverse what's happened."

"And what would these services cost me?" she asked.

"Your forgiveness for one," I said, standing and stepping out of my hiding place. I stood with my hands spread and open so that she could see me clearly and when she did, she lifted her head lightly and looked at me, not as if I were a bug to be squashed, but as if I were a life raft after a ship wreck. I walked up to stand behind the lantern and said, "I have the hatred of enough immortals. The forgiveness of one would be quite a welcomed change."

Eve sniffed again, "No tricks?"

I shook my head, "No tricks, I have a potion in my jacket pocket that will shrink you. You know the potion?"

She said that she did.

"I'm going to take it out and show you, can you promise not to squash me while I do this?"

Pulling the potion out of my jacket pocket I held it out for her to see and said, "I just need to put a drop of this on you and you will shrink back to size Eve. But we have to be careful that you don't fall down the hole while you're doing it. I'd suggest holding onto the stairs at your throne," I said pointing behind me, "That way when you shrink, you'll be safe."

She agreed and I walked in that direction as she moved her hand over the air above me and slipped her fingers behind the podium of her throne. I walked up alongside the gigantic hand and took a place beside it on the podium, I looked up at her face and asked, "Are you ready?"

Eve wiped at her eyes with the back of her other hand and took a very deep breath that echoed like wind in a cavern. She wet her lips with her tongue and said, "Thank you Donnie."

I uncorked the potion and let a drop of it fall onto her skin and quite gracefully, the Giant Queen began to reduce in size proportionately. As her hand shrank so did her arm, her upper body and Adam as well.

Soon she was at her appropriate size all things considered, she looked up at me and said, "That wasn't so bad."

I chuckled, "I honestly wasn't sure if it was going to work."

"What!?"

"Yeah," I continued unabated, "I really thought you were going to shrink around a giant Adam and split apart or something. But I'm happy it turned out alright."

"You sonofa-" she began but was cut off when above us there was an ungodly scream that shook us to our bones, she muttered instead, "Oh bollocks it's Benny."

"Sorry about this," I said to Eve as I upended half of the remaining potion onto her.

Eve gave a shriek in protest which became a long-undulated squeal as she continued to shrink until she was pocket sized. I scooped her up and slipped her into my inner pocket and ran for it just as Benny appeared over the walls and opened its horrible four segmented jaws to unleash a jet of burning green acid flames in my wake that turned the podium into a puddle.

"Cheshire, if you're going to make an appearance now would be the right time!" I shouted as I ran away from the furnace behind me and when I heard Benny dismount from the wall and give chase, knocking down the remainder of the pillars with its huge winged arms, I increased the pace but was well aware that I was heading towards a very large hole. Benny was drawing in breath just as I reached the edge and I had no choice but to fling myself out into the nothing.

Cheshire caught me in mid-air and together we crashed into a hotel bed, shattering the bedframe.

"Oh, shit that was close!" she cried out, leaping up and flattening herself against the hotel room ceiling.

I checked in my pocket, "You alive in there?" I asked.

The squeak that came out was hardly discernible but resembled something along the lines of, *"Fuck you."*

I jumped up, grabbed Cheshire's wrist and hauled her out of the room at pace and made it to the wall just as Harold rounded the corner and started shouting in fury. I pulled my knob out, pressed it to the wall, opened the door for Cheshire and kicked Harold as hard in the fork as I could before closing the door behind us.

In the dark of the antechamber the silence was total as was the colour of the light and hand-in-hand, we fumbled forwards until coming to another door. I found the handle and pulled it open and the familiar smell of Norwich rushed in like a flood.

"Welcome to my world," I said, as Cheshire stepped over the threshold of the door and I quickly followed, slamming it shut behind me.

"You took your time," Kaben said from the entrance to the alleyway and helped me fix the boards to the door again and make sure it was locked properly. Once we'd left the alleyway, we watched it seal shut behind us.

It was dawning, twilight was once again painting the city in shades of blues and grey. Alice came over, her hat under her arm and embraced Cheshire while Kaben, still wearing his rabbit mask patted me on the shoulder.

"What now?" he asked.

I checked the time on my watch, "Coffee?"

16.

It took a solid week to get through the paperwork that had piled up on my desk that Danielle had been preparing for me over the last six months. By the end of it I felt like I hadn't left at all and that perhaps the whole experience had been a mirage or a daydream.

Cheshire had moved in with Alice and Kaben and they were, wherever, having adventures and I was left to deal with hundreds of cases that needed my attention and to get back to the old daily grind.

Lilith knocked on my office door days after I had expected her to, accompanied by a heavyset fellow in a black suit and a bowler hat.

I didn't believe my eyes, "Why? Is that you?"

Kevin's monster beamed, "Indeed Mr. Rust, I'm Madam Thankeron's personal chauffeur now!"

I clapped my hands in delight, "That is incredible!"

We exchanged as many pleasantries as we could, given that he was a monster who now seemed to be better adjusted to his new life than I ever was, then he excused himself and closed my office door as he left. I heard him flirting expertly with Daniel on the other side.

"He's come a long way," I said to Lilith, proffering her a seat and sinking into my own.

"I have been very pleased with his progress," she agreed, "But I didn't come here to show him off to you."

"Oh?"

"Alice delivered the bounty to me," she said, using the word 'bounty' as a hook to see if I was going to reveal if I knew who the bounty was or not.

"She did a good job," I said, poker-faced, "Unfortunately, I spent far too much time whoring and drinking while I was there to have helped. Causing trouble is what I do."

She smiled, but it was a heavy smile.

"In case you were wondering there is nothing that can be done to help the bounty," she said, "One was made from the other and has the same genetic material...Whatever potion was used cannot be reversed and the damage is irreparable."

My passive face hurt but remained, "You're speaking of things I don't understand. As I said, I wasn't very involved in the whole matter."

"Alice did mention that you spent most of your time in the hotel," Lilith pointed out, "Causing trouble, as you said."

I sat down and started shuffling paperwork, "Yes, it was a good holiday. But I do have a lot of work to get through, Madam Thankeron, I don't wish to be rude, but I believe Danielle has your invoice ready."

Lilith smiled, nodded curtly and rose, "You know, if you want your voice fixed, we can get that seen to?"

"No need," I said, "It's just another scar."

She laughed good naturedly and moved from the chair to the door where she turned once more and asked, "Not that you were involved in anything while you were there, but hypothetically you know that the Cheshire Cat was the real Queen of Hats yes?"

I put down the papers on my desk and leaned back in my chair, "You know, hypothetically, it doesn't matter," I said, "Someone turned Wonderland into a nightmare, and I figured it was right to take that nightmare away."

"And bring it into our world?"

I laughed, a sound that no longer sounded like my laughter and gestured to the paperwork, "Into our world, yes. Thank you for the visit."

Madam Thankeron picked up my invoice at Danielle's desk and from her intake of breath I decided I had calculated the figure perfectly. After she left, Danielle appeared at the door holding up a signed cheque and said, "Not bad for a six-month vacation in Wonderland."

"I suppose you're right," I said.

"You don't seem pleased," she observed, "Bit unlike you."

I put my hands behind my head and my heels on the desk, "Oh, you know, I think I've grown as a person."

"Wow," she said, grabbing her coat, "That rabbit hole must have been really deep."

"Ask Kaben," I said, "He'd know."

END.

That Time Me and My Giant Penis Went to Hell. AKA Donnie's Inferno.
A Working Title.

Donnie is told to go to Hell, and this time, he listens.

Something is wrong down below and management have made a formal request for him to investigate. Is it because he is a skilled private investigator of the paranormal or is it because he is totally expendable?

As you would expect, Hell is almost brought to its knees in this fast paced storm of adventure. There is laughter, tears and a giant penis.
Enjoy.

A private word from the Author.

Hi there!

At the end of this novelette, I would like to take the opportunity to thank the small but remarkable audience I have who have been clamouring for me to get these works published. As any author, self-published or not, will tell you, receiving the messages encouraging us to write and publish means more than you can imagine.

For any artist it is not the grand gestures that really make a difference, but the small tokens of appreciation coming through via email, social media, letters and on one occasion a post-it note nailed to a brick.

I love you all whole heartedly and fully inappropriately. Every one of these silly, puerile, twisted and outrageously idiotic stories is written for you...
Thank you for giving me a reason to write.

Kindest Regards
Donnie Rust

PS. How cool is it that Microsoft Word can create these
☺ ☺
(.)(.) …. Nope. Didn't work.

Printed in Great Britain
by Amazon